MONSTER ROAD
by DAVID LUBAR

Other Scholastic books by David Lubar
for you to enjoy:

THE ACCIDENTAL MONSTERS series:

#1 *The Vanishing Vampire*
#2 *The Unwilling Witch*
#3 *The Wavering Werewolf*
#4 *The Gloomy Ghost*

MONSTER ROAD
by DAVID LUBAR

illustrated by
Eric Brace

AN
APPLE
PAPERBACK

SCHOLASTIC INC.

New York Toronto London Auckland Sydney
Mexico City New Delhi Hong Kong

ISBN 0-590-28168-2

Text copyright © 1999 by David Lubar.
Illustrations copyright © 1999 by Eric Brace.
All rights reserved. Published by Scholastic Inc.

SCHOLASTIC, APPLE PAPERBACKS, and associated logos are trademarks and/or registered trademarks of Scholastic Inc.

12 11 10 9 8 7 6 5 4 3 2 1   9/9 0 1 2 3 4/0

Printed in the U.S.A.   40
First Scholastic printing, October 1999

For fabulous Fred Fedorko,
a fiendishly fine friend

A Word of Thanks

Monster Road didn't start out as a book. It began as a short story about a boy who moves in with his uncle and messes up an experiment. I was happy with the story and thought it was finished. But a writer friend of mine, Elizabeth Koehler-Pentacoff, urged me to tell the rest of the tale. She wanted to read about Ned and Kevin's adventures after they left home. I'm glad I listened to her. The short story became chapter one of *Monster Road*.

But the help didn't stop there. After I wrote the book, Tonya Alicia Martin had to find time to fit it into her busy schedule at Scholastic. Without her support, this book would never have been published.

Then Michelle H. Nagler spent hours helping me smooth out the rough spots. She is a joy to work with.

And Annie McDonnell did a fabulous job uncovering those tiny little mistakes (and a few giant ones) that everyone else had missed. She kept me from looking stupid. (Not an easy task.) I give these folks my deepest thanks.

And I thank you for reading this book. I hope you like it.

MONSTER ROAD
by DAVID LUBAR

Chapter One
Uncle Ned Raises the Dead

Uncle Ned was a bit different from my other relatives. While I had aunts who loved their gardens, uncles who loved cars, and cousins who loved baseball, Uncle Ned was the only relative who had devoted himself to bringing the dead back to life. But he'd started his experiments way too late to help me. My parents had already been gone for five years before I went to live with him.

I'd been bounced around from relative to relative since the accident. I lived with Aunt Daisy for six months, until I had that problem with the heater in her fish tank. Boy, I could have used Uncle Ned's life ray that day. From Aunt Daisy, it was over to Uncle Walter, and then to Second Cousin Leo, and so on and so on through a large selection of folks I didn't

1

quite get along with. Eventually, climbing to the far end of an entire family tree, I found myself with Uncle Ned.

The previous relative, who should have known better than to leave a motorcycle sitting around with a key in it when there was a young kid like me in the house, had muttered, "You two deserve each other," as he dumped me on the doorstep of Uncle Ned's small house.

"Ah, you must be Kevin," Uncle Ned said when he answered the door. "Come on in. Let's put you to work."

With that, before I could even unzip my coat, he had me in the lab, running an experiment. Apparently, we were very close to making a breakthrough.

Life had suddenly become interesting. Life — that was the key word. Everything about it fascinated Uncle Ned. He had all kinds of books about life and death, including science books and religious books and books from other cultures. He had dead plants in pots scattered around the house. "To remind me of my mission," he told me when I asked about the withered flowers and dried-up leaves. "Life and death are separated by such a tiny spark. My goal is to find a way to restore that spark."

By the time I arrived, Uncle Ned had pretty much finished his life ray. It had gone exactly as he had planned, except for one small snag — it didn't quite work.

"We're close, Kevin," he told me on my second day there. "We are so very close. Think of it. No more death." He wandered to the front of the room and gazed out the window. I knew what he was staring at. Across the street, up the hill behind the church, was a small graveyard. Like the dead plants and the books, this also inspired Uncle Ned. After a few minutes, he turned back to me and said, "Now, let's find our next subject."

And that was the problem. Uncle Ned needed subjects. Some scientists might have bought mice or monkeys or something and killed them in order to have samples to test the life ray on. But Uncle Ned was a softie. To him, all life was special. He couldn't kill a fly. So a large part of my mission was finding freshly dead insects and animals for our experiments.

Insects were easy. Sometimes, I'd get lucky and find a small animal or a bird. Once, I found a squirrel. Whatever I found, I brought it in to Uncle Ned and he ran another test. Bit by bit, we got closer and closer. An insect would twitch and start to wriggle. It would seem almost like it was alive again. Then it would explode or burst into flame or do something else that generally isn't done by living things. Once, a bee went flying off so fast it made a hole halfway through the wall. Another time, a worm revived just long enough to tie itself into a rather messy knot.

Science is never easy.

"These life-forms are too simple," Uncle Ned said after our latest subject — a huge moth — split into several million miniature moth bits. "I know the ray would work on higher forms. We need mammals. Another squirrel, that would do the trick. I'm sure everything is working now."

So I went searching in the woods behind the house. I looked for several hours, but didn't find a single animal. I hated to let Uncle Ned down, but there just wasn't anything out there we could use. I was on my way back to the house when I spotted the rat. I could see it had been dead for more than a little while. It certainly wasn't the sort of fresh sample Uncle Ned would normally want. But it was the best I could do at the moment. Holding my breath as much as possible, I brought the carcass back to the lab.

"Ugh," Uncle Ned said when I returned. He scrunched up his nose like he had smelled — well, like he had smelled a dead rat, I guess. "Not a promising specimen."

"Sorry." I realized I'd let him down.

"Hey, don't look so sad. It's worth a try." He got out the ray and said, "I have an idea. Why don't you hook it up? Now, make sure you match the colors of the wires."

I took the various wires from the power supply and attached them to the life ray. "All set," I said when I was finished.

"Do it," Uncle Ned said.

I turned on the life ray. For a moment, nothing happened. Then the rat twitched. "Yup," Uncle Ned said as we watched, "it's bad news if the wires aren't right. I had the orange and red wires switched one time, and it was awful. The creature was a lizard, as I recall. It revived, but it was insane — full of rage and anger. Something to do with reversed polarity of the brain."

"Red and orange?" I asked, my stomach sinking through the floor. I didn't remember any orange wire — just two red ones. I looked at the back of the machine. I looked a lot more carefully than I'd looked before. My stomach sank further. I'd messed up. The orange and red wires were in the wrong plugs. A twitching caught my eye. The rat started to move. I pushed the ray aside. I knew that every second was important. The longer the ray was on, the longer the specimen seemed to remain alive.

Too late. The rat was revived, and it was angry. It gave out a little scream, then rushed right for us. "I had the wires wrong," I shouted as I backed away.

"Oh, boy." Uncle Ned tried to step between me and the rat, but he wasn't fast enough.

The rat leaped toward my face. I flinched and

thrust my hands up. Something smacked my chest. I braced for the teeth and claws. Instead, there was a thump on the floor. I looked down at the rat. It was lying motionless at my feet.

"The ray wasn't on it for long enough," Uncle Ned said. "Good thing you pushed it aside. If that rat had been beneath the ray for much longer, it might have been revived for hours."

I waited for the shouting to start.

Uncle Ned didn't shout. He smiled, then said, "I could sure go for some cocoa." He left the lab and went into the kitchen. For a moment, I just stood there, amazed that he hadn't yelled at me or thrown my stuff out on the lawn like Uncle Lester had done after I'd had that accident with the hose and gotten all those bags of concrete soaking wet. I still say he could have done *something* with them before they'd hardened.

Finally, I joined Uncle Ned in the kitchen, but I didn't say much. I felt pretty stupid making that mistake. This was definitely the sort of thing that had gotten me kicked out of more than one home.

After we'd finished our cocoa, Uncle Ned glanced toward the door. "Might as well get things cleaned up."

He went back to the lab. I followed, carrying the garbage can from the kitchen.

"Don't be so hard on yourself, Kevin," Uncle

Ned said when I joined him next to the twice-dead rat. "Everyone makes a little mistake now and then."

I was about to open my mouth when I heard a scream. It reminded me of the scream from the rat, but it sounded like it came from a larger creature. Then there were more screams — a lot of them.

Uncle Ned and I turned toward the ray. "Oh, boy," he said, pulling the plug out of the wall. "Tell me it isn't so."

I raced to the window and stared across the street. It was getting pretty active out there, up on the hill where the beam had hit. The whole cemetery was full of motion. At a lot of the graves, hands and heads were bursting through the soil. Some of the bodies had already climbed all the way out. Apparently, water wasn't the only thing that liked to go downhill. Everybody out there was heading toward the house.

A hand fell on my shoulder. I jumped. It was Uncle Ned. "Kevin, I don't know about you, but I think we're probably ready for a vacation." He reached in his pocket and pulled out his car keys. "I'd say a day or two out of town would be fine right about now." He ran upstairs, then came down a moment later carrying a suitcase.

I just stood there. How could he want me after this?

He stopped by the door. "Hey, this isn't any big

deal. Once we get on the road, remind me to tell you about the time I melted my father's car. But right now, I'd suggest we get moving."

I looked at his face. He meant it. Uncle Ned wasn't just being nice — I think he really wanted me to come.

The screams grew closer.

Uncle Ned winked, then said, "Well . . . ?"

"Sounds like a good idea." I grabbed my stuff. Most of it was still packed — I'd learned to keep it that way. I followed him to the car. Outside, screams pierced the air and some rather nasty things happened as the bodies stumbled and staggered their way down the hill. But inside, I was smiling. For the first time in my life, I had messed up and not gotten kicked out. I mean, we were leaving for a while, but we were leaving together. And then we'd both come back home. Life was really looking up.

Chapter Two
On the Road to Nowhere

Our two-day road trip ended up lasting a little longer than either of us expected. It started out normally enough — but things involving me and Uncle Ned were never called *normal* for very long. At first, however, we were quite the typical pair of tourists traveling down the highways and back roads of this great country. Okay, we were running away from a cemetery full of angry living dead, but other than that we were pretty much just like everyone else.

So it was a perfectly normal trip, until we got lost and ended up in that castle with the spooky guy who — wait, I'm getting ahead of the story.

As I said, we were on the road heading in the

best possible direction. We were heading *away* from town. Uncle Ned was telling me about melting the family car.

"I was trying to get it to run on electricity," he said. "It really should have worked. To this day, I honestly don't know what went wrong. I had two dozen batteries set up in the trunk, and I just needed to charge them. I figured they would take forever to charge if I plugged them into the wall, so I sort of tapped into the power line from the electric pole." He stopped for a moment and grinned, as if remembering the moment. Then his face got serious and he said, "Now, I don't want you to ever even think of playing with power lines. Okay?"

"Sure," I said. "I can promise you I'll never play with power lines." I'd already learned that lesson the time I tried to get Aunt Stella's Christmas lights *really* bright. Part of that whole experience is kind of fuzzy in my mind, but I believe that the jolt from the wires knocked me at least twenty feet. I probably would have gotten hurt coming down, but I was lucky enough to land on Aunt Stella. She had, as she used to say, "a fondness for sweets," and did a wonderful job cushioning my fall.

It was one of my most interesting memories. But at the moment, I had something more urgent to think about. We were in danger of ending our travels unexpectedly. I pointed toward the road ahead of us. There was a curve coming, but Uncle Ned was still looking at me.

"Curve!" I shouted, figuring that pretty much explained the problem.

"Oops," Uncle Ned said, giving the wheel a jerk and getting us back on the path. "Now, where'd that curve come from?"

"Guess whoever built the road thought it was a good idea," I said.

"Guess so," Uncle Ned said. Then he continued his story. "So, there I was with a trunk full of batteries and a line running up to the power wires. But when I plugged everything together — well, it just got really hot. It's a good thing I'd drained the gas tank first. Before I had a chance to disconnect the wires, the car got too hot to touch, and then it turned bright red. All I could do was stand and watch. Next thing I know, it's nothing but a giant puddle on the garage floor. My father was not happy."

"I can imagine," I said, settling back in my seat and watching the road whiz by beyond the side window. I was smiling. Nearly the same thing had happened to me a while back. "You know my uncle Tobias?"

Uncle Ned nodded. "Sure. I know Toby. Has a couple of kids, doesn't he? Pew and Stall? Something like that."

"Yeah, that's the one. It's Stew and Paul, I think." As their names and faces came back to me, I realized I liked Uncle Ned's version better. "I was living with him for a while, the year before last. He'd gotten his kids this radio-controlled car. I figured I could make the car run faster if I added a couple of extra batteries. I'm sure I had them wired in right. When the kids switched the car on, it just took off, heading down the road. It was a lot faster, but it didn't stop or turn no matter what they did to the controls."

"Never saw it again, did you?" Uncle Ned asked.

"Nope, it just vanished over the horizon." I laughed, remembering how the car had grown smaller and smaller as it raced down the road. Then I recalled how Uncle Tobias had yelled at me, and I didn't feel like laughing all that much.

But pretty soon after I'd told the story, we stopped for burgers and shakes, and I realized I was feeling good again. "Here," Uncle Ned said, taking the pickle off his burger and putting it on mine.

"What's that for?" I asked.

"Responsibility," he said. "If I'm taking care of you, I have to make sure you eat your vegetables."

I looked at him, wondering if he was kidding. But he had this proud expression on his face, like he'd just done a great parent-type thing. What the heck? I liked pickles. So I ate my burger, vegetables and all. Then we chased down the burgers and shakes with chocolate-marshmallow sundaes. Uncle Ned knew the importance of keeping kids fed.

When we got back in the car, Uncle Ned handed me a map. "Here, find somewhere interesting."

"Uh, sure." I unfolded the map and looked at it. Then I turned it the other way and looked at it. Neither way made much sense. To be honest, I really didn't have much experience with maps. I'd been in and out of so many different schools that I must have missed the lesson on how to read maps. But I stared at it for a while and looked at road signs and finally figured out where we were and which direction we were heading.

"See anything?" Uncle Ned asked.

"Well, there's an amusement park not far from here," I said.

"Great. Do you like that sort of thing?"

"I guess." I'd never been to one, but it sounded like a lot of fun.

"Just tell me which way to go."

So I watched the map and looked for the turns. Some of the roads didn't seem to have numbers. And some of the turns didn't quite match up with the map. But they're always building new roads, so I figured the map wasn't supposed to be exact. The day went by. We pulled off the highway and went down a bunch of long, narrow roads that ran through hills and forests. It got later and darker.

"Say," Uncle Ned asked me toward evening, "how far exactly did you say that place was?"

"I don't know. Not far." As I said it, I suddenly felt very unsure of myself. "It's just seven or eight inches. We must be getting close."

"Kevin, what's the scale of that map?"

"Scale?" I had no idea what he meant.

He reached over and pointed to the bottom of the map. "Down there. See? What does it say?"

I looked where his finger rested. There was a small bar with numbers over it. Beneath the numbers, it said something. I read it out loud. "One inch equals fifty miles." It took a second for that to sink in. It took another second to realize we were headed right toward a tree.

"LOOK OUT!" I shouted.

Uncle Ned looked up from the map and jerked the wheel. We skidded back on the road, but the car started to slide out of control. We slid across the other side, and sloshed to a stop on a muddy shoulder.

"You all right?" Uncle Ned asked.

"Yeah. You?"

"I'm fine," he said. He tried to get the car to move, but it seemed pretty well stuck in the mud. The tires spun, and the car rocked back and forth, but we didn't go anywhere.

"I have a confession," I told him after he had turned off the engine. "I'm not really very good with maps." This time, I was sure he was going to explode. It was even worse than the morning I'd tried to make a pancake breakfast for Cousin Charles and his family. How was I supposed to know they

kept salt in such a big glass jar? It sure looked like sugar to me. And even if I'd known that, I never would have guessed that salt was so bad for Cousin Charles's heart condition.

Uncle Ned patted me on the head. "I sort of guessed that just now. I have a confession, too."

"What?"

"I'm not really a very good driver."

I nodded. I had sort of guessed that, too. Even though his car was old it looked like it had almost never been used. But I didn't want him to feel bad. "I imagine it just takes practice," I said.

He nodded in agreement. "I imagine you're right. Now, we'd better figure out where we are and see about getting some help."

I stepped out of the car. Somewhere in the woods, a wolf howled. Then an owl hooted. A cloud passed in front of the full moon. The night got dark and stormy. A bat circled us, then flew off. The wind moaned. A black cat crossed our path. A clock chimed the midnight hour. Gleaming eyes peered at us from the dark. The sound of evil laughter floated toward us. Another clock chimed thirteen times. In the distance, through the trees, a light flickered in the window of a mysterious-looking castle.

"That way?" Uncle Ned asked, pointing to the castle.

"Seems fine to me," I said.

Chapter Three
Smoking Is Very Bad for the Whole Body

We stood in front of the castle. I'd never seen a castle in the middle of the woods, but I guess it was as good a place for one as anywhere else. There was no sign of a doorbell, but in the center of the door was this big metal ring hanging from a large metal bat — the kind with wings, not the kind you hit a ball with.

"Door knocker?" I asked, reaching for it.

"Seems to be," Uncle Ned said.

I hesitated. "Might be kind of late to knock," I said. Some of the relatives I'd lived with had gotten very cranky if I woke them. I really didn't want to annoy a stranger.

"I don't think we have much choice, unless you'd rather sleep in the car," Uncle Ned said.

He was right. I grabbed the knocker. Just then, the

door opened. It opened slowly and noisily, as if the hinges were rusty and the door hadn't been used for ages.

A man stood in the doorway — a tall, thin man wearing a white shirt and black pants. His face was so pale it reminded me of vanilla ice cream — not the good vanilla, but the really cheap stuff. Even his lips were pale. The only red in his face was where the whites of his eyes should have been. "Good evening," he said. "Welcome to my home."

Actually, the way he said "welcome" sounded like "velcome." But it's a lot easier for me just to tell what he said without trying to make it sound right.

"Our car is stuck by the road," Uncle Ned said. "Could we use your phone?"

"Alas, I have no phone," the man said. "I have very few modern items. You might say that I live very much in the past. But come, be my guests. I will take special care of you."

"How kind of you," Uncle Ned said. He strolled inside the castle.

I followed, happy to have found some safe shelter. The woods can be scary at night. This was much better. "Nice castle," I said, looking around.

"Why, thank you. Oh, where are my manners? I forgot to introduce myself. I am Count Sanguine, of Corpustronia." He made a low bow. As he swept his hand across his body, I noticed that he was wearing a cape. It was black on the outside, with a bright red lining.

"I'm Ned," Uncle Ned said. "This is Kevin."

"How nice to meet you," Count Sanguine said. "You are just a bit late to join me for dinner. I'm afraid I have already dined this evening." He led us through a series of halls and up a long stairway to a comfortable room with several large chairs and at least a dozen bookcases.

"Kind of dark in here," Uncle Ned said.

He was right. The place was very dim. I hadn't seen a window anywhere. We sat and talked. The count seemed happy to have visitors. He appeared almost starved for companionship. I believe he was really hungry for the sound of other humans.

As delightful as all this talking was, I started to nod off. Finally, I must have fallen asleep in my chair.

I guess I was really tired. I don't know how long I slept, but when I awoke, the count was gone. Uncle Ned was curled up in a chair next to me. There was a note on the table.

Dear Guests,
Forgive me for leaving you, but I had urgent business elsewhere. I have provided food for you. Please make yourselves at home. I will rejoin you this evening for a marvelous feast.
Count Sanguine

"How thoughtful," Uncle Ned said when he awoke and read the letter. "What a charming gentleman. You know, Kevin, there aren't a lot of gentlemen left in the world."

"Guess not." I looked around. I was starved. After a bit of searching, I found the kitchen. There was bread and cheese on a table. I brought them back to the study. They tasted wonderful.

"What about the car?" I asked as we finished our meal.

"I imagine we'll get it out soon enough," Uncle Ned said. "But what's the harm in staying for a day? The count really did seem lonely, all by himself out here in the middle of the woods. I certainly know what that's like. And I suspect he doesn't get out very much — he's so pale. What do you say we perform a good deed and give him some company?"

"That would be a nice thing to do, wouldn't it?" I looked around the room, at the walls and floor, then up at the ceiling. I thought about the count spending all his time alone in this room. That's when I got the idea. "He's been so good to us," I said. "I think we should do something for him."

"Like what?" Uncle Ned asked.

I told him my idea.

"What a wonderful suggestion," he said. "Let's do it."

So we got started on my plan. We kept at it until late in the afternoon. By then, we were tired and sweaty from all the hard work. But we had finished it and we felt great. I could hardly wait to see the look on the count's face when he found out what we'd done for him.

We collapsed in the chairs and waited for the count. He showed up just a few minutes later. "Ah," he said, "here you are. I returned very late. I was asleep, but the sound of banging awoke me. I never rise this early, but I am very sensitive to the sound of hammering. Very sensitive." He smiled. I noticed that his canine teeth were really long. I wondered if he bit his tongue much.

"Sorry about the hammering, but we have a surprise for you," Uncle Ned said.

"Ah, and I have a surprise for you," the count said, smiling even wider. His eyes almost seemed to shine. "A most satisfying surprise. A fulfilling surprise." Then he made the oddest laugh, opening his mouth very wide and curling back his lips. It really wasn't attractive. It almost looked like he was trying to bite into an invisible apple. I guess when you live alone, you pick up odd habits.

Still, I thought it was really nice that he had a surprise for us. He was being too generous. "Please, let us show you our surprise first," I said. I was so excited, I could barely stand still. Uncle Ned and I had done a great job. Besides, we had to hurry if we wanted to show him the full effect.

"By all means," the count said. "But be quick. My surprise cannot wait much longer."

"Sure." I looked toward Uncle Ned. "Show him."

"Well," Uncle Ned said. "It was Kevin's idea, but we both pitched in. To tell the truth, Kevin's a bit better with tools than I am. Anyhow, we thought that it was just so terribly gloomy in here. It's hard to be cheerful when a place is gloomy and filled with dark shadows. So look what we did for you." As he said this, he pulled the rope that was attached to the blanket covering our surprise.

It was Uncle Ned's idea to do the thing with the blanket. That way we could hide the surprise until we were ready to show it to the count.

The blanket dropped from the ceiling, exposing our handiwork. It looked great — especially considering that, despite what Uncle Ned said, I'm really not all that good with tools, either. I was glad there was still some daylight to help give the full effect.

The count gasped. It sounded sort of like "Vaht . . ." I guess he was surprised and touched by our work. He probably hadn't gotten a present from anyone in a long time.

"It's a skylight," I explained, just in case he wasn't familiar with the concept. "Think of it as a window in the ceiling. It really lets the sun in nicely, doesn't it? Well, do you like it?"

The count just stood there, staring up at the skylight. I guess he really didn't know what to say. I was proud. We'd worked hard at the surprise. We'd searched all through the castle to find the wood and the glass and the tools. It was a good thing we found what we needed upstairs. The door to the basement had been locked tight.

"Uhhhaarrgggg," the count said, still nearly speechless in surprise.

I looked over at Uncle Ned and grinned. It felt good to do something for someone else. I could tell Uncle Ned felt the same way. He was grinning, too.

"Vah . . . narggggg . . . sssssss," the count said.

Uncle Ned shrugged. "I don't recognize that language," he said. "But vah narg siss to you too."

That's when I began to notice that something wasn't right. Where the sunlight touched the count's face, smoke was rising. I guess I should have looked for a glass of water or a fire extinguisher or something, but I suspect it wouldn't have mattered. All of a sudden the count just sort of burst into flames and collapsed into a pile of ashes. In seconds, there was nothing left of the count except a tiny, smoking mound.

I looked at Uncle Ned. He looked at me. Our

special surprise really hadn't turned out the way I had hoped. "This is kind of our fault," I said, "isn't it?"

Uncle Ned nodded. Then he put his hand on my shoulder and said, "But we meant well. And, as much as I liked our friend the count, I have a funny feeling that his surprise for us might have been even less pleasant and perhaps a lot longer-lasting than our surprise for him."

"But we're still stuck in the mud and our host is a heap of ashes," I said.

"Oh, don't be so glum. I'm sure we'll think of something," Uncle Ned said. "But why don't we sleep on it? We'll think a lot better after a good night's rest."

That made sense. I looked back at the pile of ashes on the floor. "Can I make one suggestion?"

"Sure."

"Let's sleep in another room."

Chapter Four
Cutting Class the Uncle Ned Way

Using some boards left over from the skylight, and with a lot of hard work, we got the car out of the mud and back on the road. We both felt bad about turning our host into a small pile of smoldering ashes and we didn't talk a lot at first. But, after another lunch of burgers and shakes, with lots of pickles and ketchup for me, we were pretty much back to normal.

We would have headed home, but we weren't really sure where we were, thanks to my slight mistake with the map. So we just drove down the road to see where it led.

"Think of it as an exercise in serendipity," Uncle Ned said.

"What's that?"

"That's when you find something you weren't looking for," he said.

"How can you find what you aren't looking for?"

"I'm a little fuzzy on that part," Uncle Ned admitted. "But it's nice when it happens. Besides, we really can't get very lost. There has to be a town around here somewhere."

"Sooner or later." I couldn't imagine a road that didn't have a town on it somewhere. Otherwise, what was the point in having a road?

Sure enough, about a half hour later, we came to a sign that said VILLAGE OF AMLACK — 12 MILES. The sign was kind of old and rotting away, but I figured that didn't mean anything.

"Is it on the map?" Uncle Ned asked, turning toward me.

"I'll check. But maybe you should watch the road," I said, pointing in the general direction we were heading.

"Oops." He turned his attention back to his driving.

"Let's see — Amlack . . ." I looked all over the map. I couldn't find anything closer than Amesbury or Anderson. Not an Amlack anywhere. But that didn't mean a thing. I wasn't even sure if we were on the map or whether we'd gone so far we were elsewhere. I kept looking.

"Did I ever tell you about the time I sort of broke my school?" Uncle Ned asked.

"*Broke* it?"

"Yup. It was an accident, of course. So, did I tell you about it?"

"Nope. Not yet."

"Well, believe it or not, I was a bit of a goody-goody in my school days. I was always trying to impress my teachers and do things for them." He turned toward me and grinned. "Hard to believe, right?"

I nodded, pointed ahead, and said, "The road."

"Oops." Uncle Ned continued his story, while mostly keeping his eyes on the road. "One day, I decided it would make the wood-shop teacher really happy if I rigged something up to help keep the floors clean."

"Sounds reasonable," I said.

"It certainly did at the time. I really wasn't the best wood-shop student. It seems I'm a lot better at thinking about stuff than making stuff. But I had this marvelous idea for a system to clean up all the sawdust. I ran a hose from a water pipe in the basement through the floor of the shop. I attached a motor to the hose so it would sweep across the whole floor. Then I made a small hole at the other end to drain the water."

"Great," I said, hoping to speed him along in his

story. I liked his stories, but it made me a bit nervous when he told them while he was driving. He kept using his hands whenever he talked about building something. Each time Uncle Ned used his hands, he took them off the wheel. This wasn't too much of a problem when the road was straight, but it got a bit tricky along the curves.

I noticed another sign. It said AMLACK — 2 MILES.

"It *was* great," Uncle Ned said. "It cleaned the floors perfectly. Whoosh, and the wood chips and sawdust got washed away." When he said "whoosh," he shot his hand across his body like a jet whooshing across the sky. The car swerved a bit, too, but he got it back under control pretty quickly.

"Yup, got the idea," I said. "So, what was the problem?"

"Well, it seems that the ground the school was built on sort of got washed away a bit in the place where I had put the drain. I didn't notice it. Neither did anybody else. There really wasn't much to notice since the ground that was being eroded was actually *beneath* the school. After a couple of months, there wasn't anything under half of the school. That's when it just sort of broke apart."

"Snap?"

"Yeah," Uncle Ned said, "snap. Right in the middle of the day. Nobody got hurt. That was good.

But everyone was shaken up — especially the kids and teachers in the rooms along the part of the school where it broke."

"Did you get in trouble?" I asked. Out the window, I saw another sign. AMLACK — 1 MILE. GO BACK. The "go back" part seemed to have been painted on by someone. I guessed it was some kind of joke.

"Well, they weren't happy about it. But, what could they do, make me pay for it? I was just a kid. Hey, look here," Uncle Ned said, pointing ahead. "I think we've reached the village."

We were definitely approaching something. A house came into view on the side of the road. It looked pretty run-down. Another house appeared, just about as run-down as the first. I could almost hear the termites chomping away at their feast. Then there was a sign on the right side of the road. AMLACK. That's all it said. No WELCOME TO AMLACK or anything about the population or an ad for the Amlack Museum of Hand-carved Peach Pits or any other information about the place. Nothing.

Amlack itself wasn't much more than nothing. There was one main street with a couple of shops and a restaurant. Off that main street, it looked like there were some other roads with houses. But they do say that good things come in small packages, and what I saw next got my hopes up that we'd have some fun here.

"Look at him," I said, pointing to the left. The instant I said it, I knew it was a mistake, but I managed to grab the wheel and keep the car going straight while Uncle Ned joined me in staring.

"Gosh," he said, "perhaps they're having some kind of festival. That's a really fine outfit."

"Yeah. Hey, maybe we should park somewhere and walk around." I realized I'd feel better if I wasn't in a moving vehicle right now. It was distracting enough that the guy walking next to us was dressed like a pirate. Glancing up the street, I saw another guy in a cowboy outfit, complete with a gun belt and a rope. Farther on, I even thought I saw a woman wearing ancient Egyptian clothes.

I was glad that Uncle Ned wanted to stop and take a look around. Some of my relatives seemed to spend a lot of energy finding out what I liked, just so they could make sure I didn't get to do it. But Uncle Ned seemed happy to let me have fun.

"Sure, let's stretch our legs and explore." He pulled the car to the side of the road. "I guess it's okay to park here."

I looked around. "I don't see any signs. It must be okay." There weren't any other cars on the street, but I knew that if they didn't want people to park, they'd have put up some sort of warning.

We started to follow the pirate, but he went into a building. At least, I thought he'd gone in. But when we reached the spot where he'd turned, there wasn't any door. I noticed that everyone else had left the street, too. There wasn't anyone in sight.

I looked around at the shops. "Sure are a lot of antiques," I said. All the stuff that I could see through the windows of the stores seemed to be old and dusty. Some of the stuff even had cobwebs.

"I never was very interested in antiques," Uncle Ned said.

"Me, neither. Especially not after staying with Aunt Emeline. Her whole house was filled with stuff that broke when you touched it. Imagine it — everything in the place just fell apart." I shook my head, remembering that silly vase of hers. It sure had looked like it was strong enough to hold my weight. And I'd only stepped on it for a second. How else did she expect me to change that lightbulb?

I turned back to tell Uncle Ned about that unhappy event. He'd paused a few steps behind me to look in a store window. He was bent over, twirling his car keys in one hand and squinting at something in the store. And behind Uncle Ned, standing with his sword in hand, was that same pirate again. The pirate raised the sword above his head and grinned an evil grin as he stared in the direction of Uncle Ned's neck.

Chapter Five
A Spirited Adventure

Several things happened in a row. Uncle Ned lost control of his car keys and they went flying from his hand. The pirate swung the sword. I shouted, "Look out!" and Uncle Ned bent down to pick up his keys.

The sword went slicing through the space where Uncle Ned's head had been, just missing him and thunking into the wooden window frame in the front of the shop.

I guess the sword was stuck, because the pirate was yanking at it and grunting.

"Look out?" Uncle Ned asked.

I pointed behind him.

The pirate let go of the sword and ran around the corner before Uncle Ned saw him. I walked over and reached for the sword.

My hand went right through it.

"Golly," Uncle Ned said. "It must be some sort of hologram."

"Must be." I took a couple more swipes at it, then gave up. Uncle Ned was right, I decided. It was one of those laser images that look real.

Uncle Ned waved his hand through the sword a couple of times, too. "Very impressive. They really are trying to make this a special event. You'd think there'd be more visitors."

The sword got dimmer, then faded completely. I ran my hand along the window frame. There was a gash in the wood where the sword had been. I guess they really can do all sorts of things with lasers. As we turned away from the window, I saw a cowboy in front of us. He had his gun half out of its holster. And he had this look on his face like he'd been caught in the middle of doing something he shouldn't be doing. He stared at us for a second, shoved the gun back in his holster, then touched the brim of his hat and said, "Howdy, folks."

Before I could say "Howdy" back to him, he ran across the street.

"Kind of shy," Uncle Ned said.

"Maybe he feels funny about the costume," I said. I knew I'd feel strange if I had to walk around dressed up like a cowboy or a pirate.

"Perhaps he does," Uncle Ned said. "Say, here's a bookstore." He stopped and looked in the window.

I looked, too. I like books. But almost all of these were about the same sort of thing. I looked at the first book. The title was *Famous Cowards Throughout History*. The next book was *Back-stabbers and Other Villains*. There were several more, and they all seemed to be about that sort of thing, except for one called *Ghost Towns*.

"Want to go in?" I asked Uncle Ned.

"No, I'd much rather read a good science book."

"I know what you mean. This place isn't as much fun as I thought it would be."

He nodded. "When you find things you aren't looking for, you have to take your chances. You're right — this place isn't as interesting as we expected. Why don't we go back to the car?"

"Okay." As we walked away from the window, I heard a scraping sound above us. I looked up in time to see someone dressed like a Roman gladiator leaping down from the roof. He had a knife in his hand. I didn't know what he was doing, but it's a good thing we'd just moved or he would have fallen on us.

As it was, he hit the sidewalk.

"Oh, dear," Uncle Ned said. "Are you all right?"

The guy just got up and ran away.

"Must have been late for an appointment," Uncle Ned said. "But still, that's a pretty dangerous shortcut. I hope you'd never jump off a roof, Kevin."

"Nope. Not me," I said.

"Even if one of your friends did?" he asked.

I was about to tell him that I didn't have any friends, but I realized he was trying to give me some adult wisdom. This sounded like the sort of thing an adult would warn a kid about. So I told him, "I wouldn't jump off a roof just because my friends did."

"Good." He seemed satisfied with that.

We'd reached the car by then. Along the way, an arrow hit the building just behind us, a brick fell off another building, a woman dressed in Egyptian clothing offered us a bubbling drink, a man dressed as a barber waved an old-fashioned razor as he tried to talk us into coming with him for a shave, and a person dressed as a clown gave us a lit stick of dynamite. I wanted to see it explode, but Uncle Ned pulled out the fuse.

There really was a lot of activity in Amlack. It's too bad there weren't more visitors.

"It's funny," Uncle Ned said as he took out his car keys. "With all these people in costumes, you'd think the place would be more exciting." He dropped the keys again. This time when he bent over, a hatchet went flying past his head.

"Yeah. I know what you mean," I said as I walked around to the other side of the car. "The place is practically dead. But maybe this is the first time they've had a festival." I reached for the door handle.

"Here you go, dearie," someone behind me said.

I looked back. A woman dressed as a witch was holding out an apple.

"For me?"

She nodded.

"Thanks." I took it from her. She ran off. I wasn't hungry, so when I got in the car I put the apple in the glove compartment.

"Ready to go?" Uncle Ned asked as he started the car.

"Definitely. This may sound silly, but I'm glad we're leaving. There's just something spooky about this place."

I glanced in the rearview mirror. As Uncle Ned pulled out of the parking spot, a knight riding on horseback and carrying a lance went flying past. It's a good thing we'd moved, or he'd have hit us. I turned around in time to see him crashing into the side of a building.

A minute later, we were out of Amlack and heading down the road. That's when Uncle Ned surprised me by doing something that adults are always telling us is dangerous.

Chapter Six
A Small Hitch

We hadn't gone more than a few miles down the road when we saw her. She was facing us on the side of the road with her thumb out. Uncle Ned pulled over a few yards ahead of her.

"Everyone always told me it's dangerous to pick up hitchhikers," I said as I looked back.

"She's only a young girl. We can't leave her here," Uncle Ned said. "She needs a ride. She's no danger to us. And we're certainly no danger to her." He leaned toward my window and spoke to the girl. "Where are you going?"

"Just a short distance down the road," she said. "My mother lives there."

"Well, hop in," Uncle Ned told her.

I watched as she opened the back door and slid

onto the seat. Uncle Ned started to drive, then said, "Whoops." He stopped the car, then turned around and reached back, buckling the girl's seat belt. "It sticks sometimes," he said, "but safety is important."

The girl just smiled. I glanced back at her. She was kind of pretty. She was wearing a nice blue dress and she had a red ribbon around her neck. She was carrying a bouquet of flowers. I think they were daisies.

"Nice weather," Uncle Ned said as he drove down the road.

I guess he was trying to make conversation. The girl just smiled and nodded. Then her face changed. It got serious. For an instant, she looked like she was scared or in pain. It didn't last long. I felt a bit of a bump and realized we'd just driven over train tracks that crossed the road.

"What's your name?" Uncle Ned asked.

"Lucille," the girl said.

"I'm Ned, and this is Kevin." Uncle Ned turned and pointed toward me. I grabbed the wheel and held it steady until he turned back.

"Pleased to meet you," Lucille said.

I noticed that she hadn't flinched at all when the car almost went off the road. We drove in silence for a while after that. Then Uncle Ned said, "Well, Lucille, I guess you're about Kevin's age, aren't you?"

"Yeah, I guess so," she said.

I realized he was trying to get me to talk to her. I was starting to feel a bit uncomfortable. "Are we near your house?" I asked.

"Close," she said. "It's right after this next curve."

Sure enough, as we drove past the curve we saw a small house. Uncle Ned pulled into the driveway, stopped the car near the front porch, then said, "Well, here you go, Lucille. I got you home all safe and sound. I hope you don't have to hitchhike again."

She sat where she was.

"Is something wrong?" Uncle Ned asked.

"Well, I'm afraid I'll get in trouble with my mother. I'm a bit late. Could you talk to her first?"

Uncle Ned smiled at the girl. "Certainly. I understand. I'll take care of it. I'll just talk to her like one parent to another."

Parent. It was strange hearing Uncle Ned use that word, but I sort of liked it. Something deep inside me felt warm. I pushed the feeling away. I knew it never lasted.

Uncle Ned got out of the car and walked to the front door. I watched him ring the bell. A woman came to the door. "I brought Lucille home," Uncle Ned said.

The woman just stared at him for a moment. Then, so quietly I almost couldn't hear her, she said,

"Lucille's dead. She was hit by a train three years ago. She was picking daisies. She loved to pick daisies. I warned her. I told her to stay away from the tracks."

I froze in my seat. This had all seemed familiar. Then I knew. I'd heard stories like this. And I was pretty sure what would happen when I looked back. She'd be gone. There'd be something left behind — a ribbon or a flower or something, but she'd be gone.

I didn't want to look, but I had to.

I nearly jumped when I saw she was still there. She was tugging at something in her lap. I guess the seat belt was stuck. She was mumbling something, but it didn't make sense. It was something like, "Got to vanish, got to disappear." A moment later, Uncle Ned came to the car, followed by the woman.

"It happens all the time," the woman said. "People say they see her, but she always vanishes."

"Look, she's right here," Uncle Ned said.

"Lucille!" the woman shouted. She pulled the door open so fast it almost ripped off the hinges. Then she reached in and hugged Lucille so hard that the poor girl grunted.

"Here, this is a bit tricky," Uncle Ned said. He reached past the woman and undid the seat belt. "There, all better."

The woman dragged Lucille from the car, hug-

ging her and sobbing with happiness. Lucille looked stunned, like she wasn't sure what was going on.

Uncle Ned got in the car. "Good thing we came by," he said as he pulled out of the driveway.

"Yeah."

I looked over my shoulder. There was a bouquet of daisies on the seat. I guess Lucille had dropped it when her mother had given her that first big hug. I thought about telling Uncle Ned so we could return it, but I had a funny feeling we shouldn't go back there.

We drove on. After a while, Uncle Ned said, "Nice girl. Kind of quiet, but nice." He looked over toward me. "Promise me something, Kevin."

"Sure," I said. I pointed toward the road. "What?"

"Don't ever hitchhike. Okay?"

"You've got my word," I said.

"Or play on train tracks."

"Okay."

We rode for a while longer. I tried to get something on the radio, but only one channel came in, and it played nothing except spooky organ music. I started wondering about something. "Uncle Ned?" I asked.

"Yes?"

"Do strange things seem to happen to you a lot?"

"Not that I can think of. My life is pretty normal and boring. I really can't recall anything exciting. No, I'd have to say that strange things almost never happen to me."

That's when the guy with the funny red hat ran out in front of the car, waving his arms for us to stop.

Chapter Seven
Under Wraps

Uncle Ned hit the brakes, and we screeched to a halt.

"The master! The master!" the man shouted. He was so excited he was almost hopping up and down. "Help me! I beseech you. I implore you. Help me!"

He went running off the road toward a house. Well, it wasn't actually a house. It was more like a building. But it wasn't really a building, either. It was actually shaped kind of like a pyramid.

The man ran toward the door, then looked back, motioning for us to follow him. He was so excited he was almost hopping.

We pulled in next to a small car parked on the left side of the lawn.

"Guess someone needs our help," Uncle Ned said as he stepped out.

"Guess so." I got out of the car and followed Uncle Ned.

"What's the problem?" Uncle Ned asked as we caught up with the man.

"The master is trapped," he said. He was a small man, shorter than me even with the funny red hat. His eyes bulged and his voice reminded me of a voice from a cartoon I used to watch. "I am not strong enough. You must help me. I just arrived. The moving men have already gone. I thought I could handle the lid. It's too heavy. Please, this way . . ." He dashed in the front door and skittered down a hall.

"Always happy to lend a hand," Uncle Ned said.

I followed them, staring at our unusual surroundings. The place was made of big stone blocks. It was cool and damp inside — kind of like a museum. There was light coming from torches on the wall. That seemed like a really strange way to light a place.

"In here," the man said. He stopped at a door and fumbled with the latch.

"Strange hat," I whispered to Uncle Ned.

"It's a fez," he said. "Comes from Turkey."

"It's made of feathers?" I asked.

"No, not from *a* turkey," Uncle Ned explained. "It's from the country Turkey."

"Oh."

By then, the man had gotten the door open. He led us into the room. In the middle of the floor was a big stone container with a stone lid. The lid was carved to look like a person. "Please," the man said, pointing to the top.

Uncle Ned shrugged. "We'll give it a try." He and I stepped up to the lid. The three of us pushed. The lid must have weighed a ton. But it started to slide, making a shrieking sound as it grated across the rim. Finally, we shoved it far enough so it crashed to the floor.

Someone was inside.

He sat up.

"My goodness," Uncle Ned said.

I'm not sure what I said.

The guy must have had a terrible accident. Maybe that was why he'd been in a box. He was covered with bandages. I knew it wasn't polite to stare, so I looked away. I always felt uncomfortable around people who'd gotten hurt. I guess part of the reason was that it seemed to be my fault most of the time. I still felt a bit funny when I thought about Uncle Dwight and that accident with the chain saw. But even Uncle Dwight didn't have nearly as many bandages as this guy.

"A thousand blessings on you," the small man said. He smiled and bowed. "I am Ahmed Brazba-

had. This is Ramses Threp," he said, pointing to the guy wearing all the bandages.

Mr. Threp nodded. The bandages at his throat crackled like dead leaves. All I could see were his eyes. They seemed dry and old and strangely lifeless.

"I'm Ned, and this is Kevin," Uncle Ned said.

"I have other errands," Mr. Brazbahad said. "But you must stay for the night. Ramses Threp insists on it."

The bandaged head nodded again.

"Well, we'd be pleased to spend the night," Uncle Ned said. "People certainly are friendly around here. Are you sure it's no trouble?"

The man smiled again. "It would be no sacrifice for us," he said. "Please. We insist. You have done us a great favor. Let me take you to a guest chamber." He ran to the door.

As we left the room, I glanced back. Mr. Threp was climbing out of the box. He moved very slowly and he was still looking at me. I turned away so he wouldn't think I was staring at him.

Mr. Brazbahad was already far ahead of us. I didn't know why he was in a hurry, but I jogged to catch up with him.

"Why do you call that guy 'master'?" I asked when I reached him.

"Ah, a slip of the tongue," he said. "Ramses Threp is my client. I arrange for the transportation of people and items. Ramses Threp desired to leave his home in Egypt and spend time in your wonderful land. I aided him in his trip. That is all. My work is done. As a matter of fact, I will be leaving shortly. Yes, I will be gone before long. I have other tasks to carry out for the master."

"You just called him 'master' again," I said.

"No, I didn't." He stopped in front of another door. "Ah, here we are. A special room for special guests."

I wanted to ask about the bandages, but I figured that would be rude. So I didn't say anything and just went into the room. It was very nice. There was one tiny window, barely more than a slit near the very top of the wall. A spot of sunlight came through it, striking the floor near the corner. There were fancy tapestries on the walls, and all these really great statues of cats.

"A cat lover," Uncle Ned said as he looked around the room.

Mr. Brazbahad nodded, getting dangerously close to losing his fez. "Ramses Threp is quite fond of cats. He would cut out your very own — I mean *his* very own heart to help a cat. Now, please make yourselves comfortable. You will find everything you need in this room." He waved his hand around, then pointed to a row of clay jars along one wall. "You will find food — enough food for a long journey."

"That's very kind of you," Uncle Ned said.

"My pleasure." Mr. Brazbahad bowed. "Now, I must hurry to my appointment."

I waited for his fez to fall off, but it stayed on. Maybe he used some kind of glue or hair wax. Or maybe it worked like a suction cup. He kept bowing as he backed out of the room.

"Well, thanks again," Uncle Ned said to Mr. Brazbahad. "We consider ourselves lucky to have found a place for the night."

"Or perhaps even longer," Mr. Brazbahad said, making one final bow before he stepped out of the room. A moment later, I heard the sound of car tires screeching as someone drove away real fast. I guess Mr. Brazbahad wasn't kidding when he said he was in a hurry to leave.

Chapter Eight
Have a Knife Evening

"Nice fellow," Uncle Ned said.

"Yeah, but I wonder what happened to that other guy. He must have been in a really bad accident."

"Now, Kevin, if he wanted us to know, he would have told us."

"I guess." I looked around the room. "Hey, there's no mattress on the bed." I walked over to the middle of the room. This was definitely the strangest bed I'd ever seen. It actually looked like nothing but a big block of stone with some designs carved on it. "Talk about rocking yourself to sleep. And with a real rock . . ."

"We'll be fine," Uncle Ned said.

I shook my head. "It doesn't look very comfortable." I decided to examine the rest of the room. As I moved away from the bed, I heard a loud rumbling. I was startled for a second until I realized it was only my stomach making the noise and there was no danger of the room falling apart. I walked over to the row of jars and picked one up. It was sealed on the top with a piece of clay.

"Snack time?" I asked Uncle Ned.

"Huh?" He looked up from the floor. I guess he'd been studying something. He pointed to the spot of sunlight in the corner. "Fascinating," he said. "If you follow the path, it goes right to here." He went over and put his finger on a spot on the middle of the stone slab.

I joined him and studied the markings. There was a drawing of the sun, surrounded by all sorts of symbols. There was a cat and a knife and a heart. But I was more interested in filling my stomach. "Yeah, fascinating. Do you think it's okay if I open one of these jars?"

Uncle Ned nodded. "Mister Brazbahad did offer food to us."

"Great." I broke open the top of the vase. It was funny breaking something when I had permission. It felt really strange. Usually, I broke stuff when I wasn't planning it. Like the time I had tried decorating the Christmas tree with all of Aunt Florence's ceramic birds.

I reached into the vase and pulled out a loaf of bread. It wasn't my idea of a perfect snack, but it would do. I'd eaten a lot worse. I still gag every time I think of the two months I lived with Cousin Ellen. All she ate was vegetables. That wouldn't have been so bad, but the only vegetables she ate were the ones she found growing by the side of the road. Every day she'd go out jogging and come back with weeds for dinner.

I tried to break off a piece of bread, but it was really hard. "I think this is pretty old," I told Uncle Ned.

"Let me try." He took the bread and did his best, but he couldn't break it, either. He shook his head. "I think we need a knife."

"I'll go look for one." I felt like exploring a bit, anyhow.

"Fine." Uncle Ned returned his attention to the spot of sunlight. It had moved partway across the floor, getting closer to the stone bed.

I went out into the hall and looked around. There was a slow, scraping sound coming from far off to the left. It was like someone was rubbing sandpaper on a sidewalk — but it was real slow. There was a long scrape, then a pause, then another scrape.

I went all the way down the corridor and turned the corner before I found what was making the noise. "Oh, hi," I said. Our host, Mr. Threp, was walking toward me. He was carrying a knife. I guess he'd figured out we'd have a problem with the bread. "Hey, thanks," I said. I ran up, grabbed the knife from him, and headed back to the room.

He didn't say anything, but I figured it was hard to talk with all those bandages.

"Got it," I said when I came back into the room. I picked up the loaf of bread and tried to figure out where to start cutting.

"Here, better let me do that," Uncle Ned said. "Wouldn't want you to get hurt."

I gave him the knife. As soon as he tried to slice the bread, he cut himself.

"Yeowch," Uncle Ned said, holding up his hand.

Some kids can't stand the sight of blood. But I'd seen a fair amount of it — a lot of my relatives seemed to get hurt when I was around. I guess we're sort of a clumsy family. Anyhow, the blood didn't bother me. It didn't look like a serious cut, but it was a bit messy. I searched the room for something to use to stop the bleeding.

"Golly, I really seem to have sliced myself," Uncle Ned said.

"Yeah. I'll be right back."

I ran out the door. Mr. Threp was still coming down the corridor. He'd reached the corner by now, but he was going pretty slowly. I ran to him. "I need a bandage," I said.

He raised his arms toward me. It almost looked like the way people stand when they're pretending to walk in their sleep. He just stuck both hands straight out. For a moment, I wasn't sure what he wanted, but then I saw a piece of bandage dangling from his right hand.

"Great," I said, grabbing the bandage. "Thanks." I turned and ran back to Uncle Ned.

Behind me, I think Mr. Threp started to say something. But it wasn't very clear, and I really didn't have time to stand around while Uncle Ned was bleeding all over the place.

"Here," I said when I got back. I took his hand and wrapped the end of the bandage around it a couple of times, putting pressure on the wound, just like I'd done with Uncle Harold's foot after that time when he'd tried to teach me how to split wood with an ax.

In a minute, the bleeding stopped.

"Thank you, Kevin," Uncle Ned said. He looked at his hand, then down to the floor. "Gosh, that's a long bandage."

I followed his gaze. The piece I'd brought trailed back out the door. "Mister Threp gave it to me," I said. I picked up the knife and cut the bandage so it wouldn't be dangling from Uncle Ned's hand.

"Well, we'd better go thank him."

"He's right down at the end of the hall," I said.

"I think he was on his way here, but he walks pretty slowly."

"So, let's go meet him," Uncle Ned said.

I walked out with him and we went down the hall, picking up the bandage as we went. The piece stretched all the way along the corridor to the corner. The other end was lying on the ground right about where Mr. Threp had been. But there was no sign of him. It was like he had vanished.

"He was here a minute ago," I said. I looked around the corner. There was nobody in sight. I looked at the floor. There was something down there. I knelt. There were two round things. They looked like eyes. But that made no sense. I got back up.

"Perhaps he's shy," Uncle Ned said. "Maybe he feels funny about his appearance."

"Maybe," I agreed. "Well, how about I slice some bread for us?" My stomach was really rumbling now.

"Sounds good to me," Uncle Ned said.

We went back to the room. A while later, the spot of sunlight reached the place on the bed where the carved sun was. I waited for something special to happen, but nothing did. I guess it was just a decoration after all.

I slept pretty soundly that night, even though the bed was hard. There was no sign of Mr. Threp the next morning. Uncle Ned and I looked for him so we could thank him for his hospitality, but he didn't show up.

"Guess he's busy somewhere," Uncle Ned said.

"Yeah, he's probably wrapped up doing something," I said.

We slipped out the front door and got back into the car.

Chapter Nine
A Sticky Situation

"What do you say?" Uncle Ned asked. "Should we keep going this way or try to find our way back home?"

"Keep going," I said. I really liked the fun of just heading somewhere without knowing where we would end up. Besides, I was supposed to be in charge of the map and I didn't have any idea at all how to get back home. I didn't want Uncle Ned to know how badly I'd messed up.

"Onward," Uncle Ned said. He started the car and pulled onto the road. "You know, this is fun. And I can't remember the last time I took a vacation."

"I can," I told him. "Aunt Irene and Uncle Oscar took me camping once. Did you know that if you leave a cooler open, the food attracts bears?"

"That makes sense," Uncle Ned said.

"Did you know that Aunt Irene can run faster than Uncle Oscar?" I asked.

Uncle Ned nodded. "That makes sense, too. I can just see her running right over the poor guy."

I laughed, remembering the sight of the two of them racing through the woods. Uncle Oscar had started out in the lead, but he'd stumbled and Aunt Irene had pretty much used him as a springboard. I'd just stayed in the tent. After all, the bears already had the food, so there was no reason for them to bother me. But I guess my aunt and uncle had seen it differently. They weren't real happy on the drive back from that vacation. It had been pretty quiet in the car. All they'd talked about was which relatives might love to have a certain boy come live with them.

"Well, none of that matters. We're both having a great vacation now," Uncle Ned said.

"Yeah." *So far,* I thought. Things started out great lots of times, but something always happened. I did something wrong or hurt someone or broke something. I'd gotten pretty used to it over the last few years, but now I'd found a person I really wanted to stay with. I promised myself I'd be extra careful.

A while later, we spotted a small store with a gas

pump in front. "Better fill up," Uncle Ned said as he pulled up to the pump. "Why don't you run in and pick out something for lunch."

"Okay." I got out of the car and went into the store. There was nobody behind the counter. "Hello?" I called out, looking around. The place was empty. It was kind of messy, too. There were all these small, sticky blobs on the floor. I found some sandwiches in one of the cases, and grabbed a couple of cartons of chocolate milk. It's important to get enough of the dairy group — especially the chocolate dairy group.

"There's nobody out there," Uncle Ned said as he came in through the door.

"Nobody in here, either," I said.

Uncle Ned looked at the stuff I'd gotten. "Well, let's leave the money for the food and gas on the counter."

"Okay." I waited while Uncle Ned totaled the stuff up and put some money down. Then we went out. In front of the store, there was a wooden table like the kind they use for picnics. We sat on a bench and ate our lunch. Nobody showed up.

"Might as well get back on the road," Uncle Ned said.

"Yeah." I got up. "Hang on a second," I said. I walked to the side of the building, where there was a door for the bathroom. "Be right back."

When I went in, I almost tripped over something. It was somebody's clothes — pants, shirt, socks, underwear, and shoes, just lying there like the person had been sucked right out of them. The shirt was one of those blue ones with the person's name sewn on above the pocket. In red thread against a white patch, it said LUCKY.

Must be a nickname, I thought. But it was strange that Lucky had left his clothes there. I stepped over the clothes and went to the toilet. There were more of those blobs on the floor. I also saw some of the stuff inside one of Lucky's shoes. It almost seemed to be moving. I tried to wash my hands in the sink. But as soon as I bent over, this weird stuff started coming up from the drain. It was some sort of thick, dark blob. It looked like the stuff on the floor, but there was a lot more of it.

I knew what was going to happen. Uncle Ned would come in next, and he'd see this blob, and he'd blame me. He'd think I'd been fooling around and clogged up the sink. Maybe I had clogged up a sink or two in the past. There was that time at Aunt Pattie's when I'd wanted to play with a boat in the sink but the drain wouldn't close so I'd stuffed it with paper towels. I'd started the water running and then I'd gone to look for my boats. I guess something had distracted me, because I'd forgotten to go back to the bathroom and shut off the water. It wouldn't have been so bad if it had been a downstairs bathroom, but when the water overflows upstairs, it sure has a lot of places to run.

"Everything okay in there?" Uncle Ned called from outside.

"Yeah, I'll be out in a second."

Whatever was clogging this sink, it wasn't my fault. But I really didn't want to get into trouble with Uncle Ned. There was a mop in the corner of the bathroom. I grabbed it and used the handle to push at the blob. I expected it to go down, but the darn stuff started to climb up the handle. It almost got to my hand before I dropped the mop. When stuff fell off the end of the handle, I noticed that some of the wood had been dissolved.

"I have to get rid of this," I muttered as I looked around. There was a plastic container under the sink. The label said DRAIN CLEANER. I knew that the stuff was dangerous. It was strong enough to take the paint off a car — as I had found out by accident at Uncle Fritz's house. He sure had acted like a baby when it came to that car. I picked up the bottle and opened it.

"This should do the trick," I said. I leaned as far away as I could to avoid the splashes and started to pour. Wow. The second the stuff hit the clog, the whole thing started to sizzle. Then it all started pulling back down the drain. Whatever they made

the drain cleaner with, it really worked. I wasn't sure how much to use, so I kept pouring. Before I knew it, the bottle was empty. When I was done, I leaned over and looked into the sink. There was no sign of any clog.

The air in the bathroom smelled a bit funny. "Sorry about the stink," I said to Uncle Ned as I opened the door.

"No need to apologize," he said as he stepped past me into the bathroom. "It's all just part of being human." But he came right out, then started opening and closing the door to fan the air.

"I warned you," I said.

"Maybe we need to pay a bit more attention to your diet, Kevin," he said. He took a deep breath, then went back in.

I waited outside for him. When he was done, we returned to the car and drove away from the store. I hoped there was something interesting up the road. I was ready for a bit of excitement.

Nothing much happened that afternoon. We kept driving down the road. I didn't have to worry about the map — we never came to a single turn. The road just went on, winding through hills and woods, going over a stream once in a while or crossing train tracks. It was a nice ride, and Uncle Ned was great company — except that I still had to keep an eye on his driving when he was talking.

Toward the end of the afternoon, it started to get foggy. By early evening, we'd slowed down a lot. The road was only visible for a short distance. Even though we hadn't seen a single car coming in our direction, Uncle Ned had to be careful to stay on his side of the road just in case.

"I think there might be something up ahead," he said as the last of the daylight faded.

"Yeah, it looks like another town."

The road changed from asphalt to cobblestones. We drove past some small houses. "I suspect we'd be better off walking," Uncle Ned said. He pulled over to the side of the road and we got out.

"There," I said, pointing ahead. Through the fog, I could just make out a building with a large wooden sign hanging in front.

We walked closer. I could tell it was some kind of restaurant. When we got right under the sign, I was able to read it: THE INN OF THE BLACK RAVEN. FOOD AND LODGINGS.

I followed Uncle Ned through the door. There was a man wiping one of the large wooden tables with a rag. "Evening, gents," he said, greeting us with an English accent. I looked around the place. It was just like one of those inns you see in movies about England.

"Kevin," Uncle Ned asked, peering around the

room, "do you remember us crossing any large bodies of water? An ocean, perhaps?"

"Nope. Just a couple of streams."

Uncle Ned shrugged. "That's odd," he said. He sat at a table, then said, "Well, the main thing is that we're safely out of the fog."

"Yeah," I agreed. "It was a little scary there for a while, but the worst is behind us."

"Good thing you got here when you did," the man said as he walked over to our table. "I was just about to bar the door. It's not safe to be about, what with the full moon coming and that murderous beast on the prowl."

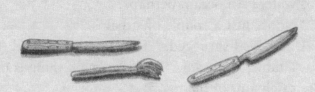

Chapter Ten
Fur Crying Out Loud

"Beast?" Uncle Ned asked.

"Aye," the man said. "There's a beast comes out when the moon rises full. Some say it's part man and part wolf. And the unlucky traveler who meets it, why he'll get ripped to shreds by the beast. He'll have his arms and legs torn off and his liver and heart pulled dripping from his mangled body." He paused to take a pad and pencil from his pocket, then said, "Now, what can I get you to eat?"

Uncle Ned looked around the room for a moment, then said, "Well, most inns like this make a pretty good T-bone steak. Would you have one?"

The man nodded. "We would, sir. And it's very tasty." He glanced over at me. "And for you, lad?

Some blood sausage, perhaps, or a nice juicy plate of tripe?"

"What's tripe?" I asked Uncle Ned, figuring it had to be better than blood sausage.

"It's the lining of a cow's stomach," he told me. "It's quite delicious if you don't think about it too much."

I shook my head, swallowed, then said, "You know, I have this sudden craving for a salad."

"Very well. Let me just bar the door and I'll get started on your food." He walked toward the wooden door at the front of the room.

As he reached it, the door flew open and a man hurried in. The wind shrieked at his back, tearing through the room. "Not a fit night for a man or beast," the man said in a roaring voice, nodding to the innkeeper. "Glad I found you open."

"Welcome, sir," the innkeeper said. He stepped past the man, shut the door, and put a wooden bar in place. "That will keep the beast out," he said, "though the only real protection is a silver bullet." He walked around the room closing and locking all the shutters on the windows.

"Ah, fellow travelers," the man said. He strolled to our table and looked at one of the empty chairs. "May I?"

"We'd be delighted," Uncle Ned said.

The man sat down. "Innkeeper," he called, "a

steak, and make it so rare it's still moving." He grinned, then turned toward us. "I'm Lord Howel," he said.

"I'm Ned, and this is Kevin," Uncle Ned told him.

"Lovely night," Lord Howel said, looking toward the door. "If I'm not mistaken, the full moon should be rising soon. A lovely sight, it is. Now, may I ask what brings the two of you to this lonely spot?"

"We're just traveling," Uncle Ned said.

"Any relatives at home?" the man asked. "Anybody to wonder where you've gone?"

"Nope. Just the two of us," Uncle Ned said.

The man nodded. "How delightful. I hope you enjoy your travels. I'm here for some sport. I do so love to hunt. You could say it's in my blood." He laughed, displaying the whitest teeth I'd ever seen. Then he paused and scratched his neck very fast with his right hand, making rapid up-down movements.

After he'd finished scratching, Lord Howel stared at us for a moment, then said, "Meat."

"What?" Uncle Ned asked.

"I'm pleased to meet the two of you," Lord Howel said.

He turned his head toward the kitchen and sniffed. A moment later the innkeeper came out with our food. I know it's not nice to say bad things about adults, but Lord Howel was certainly not the neatest eater I'd ever seen. He grabbed the steak with his hands and started ripping it with his teeth.

I looked at Uncle Ned. He shrugged and winked at me. Then he dug into his pie. I'd lost my appetite, but I managed to eat part of my salad. At least the vegetables didn't look like they'd been picked from the side of the road.

While Lord Howel ate, he kept staring at Uncle Ned and me. I noticed that the backs of his hands were very hairy. I also noticed that he only had one eyebrow, which ran all the way across his forehead.

Uncle Ned finished his food, then pulled out his wallet. He took out some money and said to the innkeeper, "So, what do we owe you for this wonderful meal?"

The innkeeper stared at Uncle Ned's hand. "What's that?" he asked.

"Money," Uncle Ned said, looking puzzled.

"Not around here," the innkeeper said. "Gold coins are all we take. Where do you think you are?"

Uncle Ned opened his mouth, then sighed and said, "I'm afraid that's all we have."

"Then you'll be washing dishes tonight," the innkeeper said. He pointed to the kitchen.

Uncle Ned got up. I followed, glad to get away from Lord Howel and his bad table manners. I glanced back. It was even worse now. He'd dropped to his hands and knees on the floor, taking his steak

with him, and had started groaning and making snarling sounds. I guess when you're a lord, you don't have to worry about what other people think of you.

"I don't mind washing dishes," I told Uncle Ned as we went through a door into a small kitchen. A stack of dirty dishes towered over a sink against the far wall. "I've done it a lot. I used to help with the dishes all the time at Cousin Willie's house, but he got kind of tired of me dropping stuff. I never could figure out why they make kitchen floors so hard. I told him he should put a rug in the kitchen, but he didn't think that was a good idea."

"So," Uncle Ned asked, "wash or dry?"

"Dry."

We got to work. Uncle Ned started washing the dishes and the forks and spoons and knives. He handed them to me to dry. It was actually kind of nice — it felt like a family thing. I was extra careful with the dishes. Even though they didn't belong to Uncle Ned, I really didn't want to break any of them. I was careful with the knives and forks, too. They were very solid and heavy. They looked expensive.

"Interesting man," Uncle Ned said, pointing toward the door that led to the main room of the inn.

"Yeah. I wonder what he's planning to hunt."

There was a shout from the other room. "THE BEAST!" It sounded like the innkeeper. Then he said it a couple more times: "The beast! The beast!"

Uncle Ned shook his head. "Looks like he's still telling everyone about it. Maybe it's a local custom. I guess he likes to entertain the diners."

"He really does like to talk about it." As I finished drying the silverware, I heard the sound of furniture crashing in the other room. Then there was a smashing sound, like a glass had been broken. *Lord Howel must really be making a mess in there,* I thought. I remember seeing a movie where some people had thrown their glasses into a fireplace. Maybe that's what he was doing.

There were a couple more crashes. "Quite a celebration," Uncle Ned said.

I looked down at the knives and forks. "What should I do with these?"

He glanced around the kitchen and shrugged. "Might as well take them into the dining room."

"Okay." I put the silverware on a tray and went toward the door. As I got there, I could hear the innkeeper still shouting about the beast, and I could hear the sounds of more crashing and smashing. I really didn't understand how he expected people to come back when he made such a fuss. But that was his business.

I stepped through the door. Right at the same time, the innkeeper came rushing in from the other direction. I had to dodge to the side to avoid crashing into him. Unfortunately, I lost my balance and started to stumble. I also lost my grip on the tray. As the tray fell to the ground, I shot my hands out. I was a bit clumsy about it and only managed to knock the tray so it went tumbling away from me.

All the knives and forks shot off the tray and went sailing through the air. Now here's the strange part. As I looked into the room, I saw Lord Howel flying toward me. Actually, he was leaping more than flying, but he was coming really fast. He was moving so fast he was almost a blur. He looked a lot hairier than I'd remembered, but the light wasn't very good in the inn, even with the beams of the full moon coming through the slits in the shutters.

Maybe Lord Howel would have escaped from harm if he hadn't leaped so fast. But between his speed and the speed of all the silver knives and forks, there was quite a collision. He dropped to the ground, looking like a giant, hairy pincushion. He let out this really awful scream, then turned and jumped right through one of the shuttered windows, crashing to the ground outside.

"Everything okay out there?" Uncle Ned asked, peering in from the kitchen.

"I guess." I looked past Uncle Ned. The inn-keeper was huddled in a corner of the kitchen. I went back over to him. "Listen, I'm sorry about the forks and stuff. I mean, I didn't run off with them — that Lord guy did — but I guess it was sort of my fault. So, I'm sorry."

The innkeeper looked up at me. He seemed about to say something. Then his eyes rolled back and he slumped over. He'd fainted. I knew what that looked like because Aunt Velma fainted that time when I'd lost my corn snake and it had showed up in the laundry hamper. Of course, she'd been standing at the time, so she made a bit more of a thump when she went down. At least the innkeeper was already on the ground.

I knew what to do. I threw some water on his face. That woke him up, but he just kept saying stuff about the beast.

There didn't seem to be much else Uncle Ned and I could do, so we went up and found a room. The next morning, the innkeeper looked a bit better, but we still couldn't get him to talk. He did bring us some breakfast, but he just kept mumbling about the beast the whole time he was serving us. At least when Uncle Ned tried to pay him again, he shook his head.

"Might as well get back on the road," Uncle Ned said. "This place doesn't seem too interesting."

"I'm ready," I said.

When we got outside, we saw that the fog had lifted. It looked like it would be a beautiful day. As we walked to the car, I noticed a couple of forks lying on the road, then some more forks and knives leaving a trail toward the woods. "I'm definitely ready," I said, getting into the car.

We headed off, all set to enjoy another lovely day. Pretty soon, the cobblestones ended and the road turned back to asphalt. We'd only gone a few miles when Uncle Ned got this worried look and said, "Uh-oh." Then he pulled the car to the side of the road and said, "Trouble."

Chapter Eleven
Statues Pose a Question

"What's wrong?" I asked.

"I think we have a flat tire."

That was a relief. Our last few problems had been strange enough that I'd started getting ready for anything. If the road had suddenly turned into the back of a brontosaurus or the trees had started walking, I wouldn't have been surprised. But this — a flat tire — was a nice, simple problem that we'd have no trouble dealing with. The only real danger was if the jack slipped when someone was under the car. And that had only happened once when I was around. And, considering what a mess it had been, the doctors had really done a good job fixing Uncle Roy's face.

I hopped out of the car as soon as it stopped.

Sure enough, the right front tire was flat. Uncle Ned took a look at it, then said, "Well, as the old joke goes, it's only flat on the bottom." He opened the trunk and handed me the tire iron.

"See if you can get the hubcap off," he said.

I put the end of the bar against the edge of the hubcap and pried it loose. It popped right off. The polished chrome hubcap spun on the ground for a moment before it clattered to a halt. I tried to loosen the lugs on the tire. But they were real tight.

"Wait, I have a better idea," Uncle Ned said. He took something else out from the trunk and showed it to me.

"Instant tire in a can?" I asked, reading the label.

"Compressed air and something to seal the hole. Isn't science great?" Uncle Ned turned the can in his hand and started reading the directions.

I decided to stretch my legs. I wandered off the side of the road among the trees. I expected to see nothing but woods. Instead, I found myself at the start of a huge collection of statues. "Hey, Uncle Ned, come look at this."

I heard him stumble through the woods behind me. "Gosh, who'd have thought this would be here," he said.

We just stood where we were, amazed by what we saw. There were statues all around the trees.

There were lots of people, but there were also squirrels and dogs and birds. As much as I usually protested when any of my relatives took me to a museum, this was really interesting. I especially liked the faces of the statues. They had their eyes wide open, as if they were startled. Some of them were shouting, too.

We wandered around for a while, enjoying the artwork. Every once in a while, I heard this strange sound, as if someone was following us. But I didn't see anybody.

"Well, maybe we should push on," Uncle Ned said.

So we went back to the car. He picked up the can, then looked at me and said, "Want to give it a try?"

"Sure." It seemed like it would be fun. I took the cap off the tire stem, then pressed the valve of the can against the stem. There was a hissing and the tire started to inflate.

"Hey, it's working." I watched as the tire rose and the flat edge turned round. "How do I know when to stop?" I asked.

"It tells you on the side of the can," Uncle Ned said.

I tried to turn the can so I could read it while I was still putting the stuff inside the tire. I guess that was a mistake. All of a sudden, stuff was squirting all over the place. It hit me in the face. I think it also hit Uncle Ned.

"Oh, dear," he said. "I got some in my eyes."

I had some in my eyes, too. I could barely see. But there was a roll of paper towels in the backseat of the car. I opened the rear door and fumbled around until I felt it.

Behind me, I heard a sudden hissing. It startled me and I dropped the towels. For a moment, I thought the tire was leaking again. It was a loud hiss, but I realized it didn't seem to be coming from near the tire.

"What's that?" I asked.

"I don't know," Uncle Ned said. "I can't see."

"I'll get the towels," I told him. I felt around. My hand hit something hard. I picked it up. The hissing was coming closer. It actually sounded like a bunch of little hisses instead of one big one. But that didn't make any sense. The thing I'd touched was smooth and hard. I turned it around in my hand. I couldn't see much, except flashes of sunlight reflecting off a shiny surface.

"The hubcap," I said. I held it in front of me for a second, wondering where I should put it so it wouldn't get lost. Right then, I could have sworn I heard a woman scream.

I think that's when the hissing stopped. All of a sudden, it was just gone. I put the hubcap down and

felt around on the ground some more. "Here they are," I said when I found the towels. I pulled one off to wipe my eyes, then gave the roll to Uncle Ned. In a couple of minutes, we were both as good as new.

"I'm sorry," I said. "I wasn't trying to squirt us. I just turned the can the wrong way. It was an accident."

"I know, Kevin," Uncle Ned said. He put his hand on my shoulder. "No harm done. Stop worrying about it. And the tire is fixed. Besides, we also got to see some fascinating sculptures. Though I must say, I don't care for that one."

When I looked where he was pointing, I almost jumped. Just next to us, a few feet away, was this incredibly ugly sculpture of a woman with snakes for hair. I didn't remember seeing it earlier. As a matter of fact, I'm almost positive it hadn't been there when we first arrived. But that couldn't be. I guess I just hadn't noticed it before.

"Now that's ugly," I said.

"It looks like Medusa," Uncle Ned said.

"Who?" I asked.

"She's a character in a Greek myth," he told me. "They say she was so ugly, anyone who looked at her turned to stone."

"What a silly story. How could anyone believe that?"

I picked up the hubcap from the ground. It really was shiny. I could see myself in it. I made a few ugly faces, but gave up right away. Compared to the statue, nothing I could do would be even a little bit hideous.

I walked over to the statue and held the hubcap up in front of her eyes. "If you could see yourself," I said, "you'd probably scream." I turned away from the statue and put the hubcap on the wheel. This had been a nice break, but I was ready to get back on the road.

Unfortunately, Uncle Ned started telling me a story as soon as we got in the car. So he wasn't watching very carefully when he pulled onto the road. He sort of swerved a bit and hit the statue of the lady with the snakes in her hair. She toppled over. But I didn't think anybody would really mind. It was such an ugly statue.

Once again, the road ran along with no other roads crossing our path. That made my job with the map pretty easy. All I had to do was sit back and relax and watch the sights pass by. But I was positive by now that, wherever we were, it wasn't on the map — at least, not on the map that we had.

"Nice woods," Uncle Ned said, glancing around as he drove along the tree-lined route.

"Yeah, reminds me of Cousin Edward's place," I said, remembering the week I had stayed there.

"How is Edward?" Uncle Ned asked.

"Not too good, at least the last time I saw him."
I flinched a bit as I thought about my brief stay with
that cousin.

Uncle Ned looked over at me. "Something happen?"

I pointed toward the road and waited until Uncle Ned had turned his eyes back to the upcoming
curve. "Well, he lived in this nice house near the
woods. And there were all these weeds at the back of
his lawn. One day, while he was off at work, I figured I'd clean things up. I'm a pretty good worker
when I have something to do."

"I know you are," Uncle Ned said.

"I found some gardening gloves and some tools.
I spent the whole day cleaning up. The backyard
looked great when I was done. I was just putting the
last of the weeds into some trash cans when Cousin
Edward got back from work. He came over to see
what I was doing and he was real happy. The first
thing he did was push down all the leaves that were
in the cans so there would be more room." I paused
for a minute, remembering the scene. It was sum-
mer, and Cousin Edward had been wearing a short-
sleeved shirt. I could still see him, pushing down on
all those weeds, getting all the way up to his elbows.

"Sounds like he was very pleased."

"He was," I said. "At least, until he took a good
look in the cans." I shrugged. "Hey, I hadn't spent a

lot of time in the woods. How was I supposed to know what poison ivy looked like?"

"Good thing you were wearing gloves," Uncle Ned said.

I nodded. "Yeah, I guess that was good. But Cousin Edward didn't do too well. By the time I left, he looked pretty much like something from a horror movie."

"Like the Blob?" Uncle Ned asked.

"What's that?"

"Big jellylike creature. It went around absorbing people and growing bigger. Crawled around in sinks, hiding in the drains."

I shook my head. "Never heard of it."

"Well, you really can't blame yourself about the poison ivy," Uncle Ned said.

I was about to answer, but we'd just gone over the top of a hill, and the scene in the distance got my attention.

"Now that's impressive," Uncle Ned said. He slowed the car so we could both take a good look before going down the hill.

"Yeah. Maybe it's an airport." I saw five large buildings spread across an area surrounded by a fence. There were also five towers and a huge radar dish.

"No landing strip," Uncle Ned said. "So I don't think it's an airport. I suspect it's some kind of research lab." He grinned. "Now that's my idea of fun."

I nodded. "Maybe they have tours." I had a feeling it could be interesting. At the very least, they'd be able to tell us where we were.

We headed down the hill, losing sight of the place for a while. Then we went around several curves. Finally, we reached a spot where there was a fence running next to the road. I noticed strands of barbed wire on top of the fence.

"Must be an entrance somewhere along this fence," Uncle Ned said.

Sure enough, we came to a gate a minute later. There was a sign on it: KEEP OUT.

Uncle Ned drove up to it. The gate swung open.

"What about the sign?" I asked.

"We're scientists," he said. "I'm sure we'll be welcome. That sign is just for the public. Some places don't want to be annoyed by visits from the public. But scientists are all part of the same universal community. I'm certain we'll be welcomed with open arms."

"You sure it's okay?" I asked.

"Positive," Uncle Ned said. "We just have to find whoever is in charge of greeting visitors."

That's when the men with the guns ran up to the car. One of them shouted, "HALT!"

Uncle Ned stopped the car and looked around. "On the other hand," he said, "some places are a bit stricter about security than others."

Chapter Twelve
Who Ray?

The guards, who were wearing uniforms with the letters *GWI* on them, took us out of the car and herded us down a path toward a large building.

"I'm a member of the National Association of Independent Scientists," Uncle Ned told them.

They didn't say anything to him.

"We can come back when you aren't so busy," I said.

They didn't say anything to me, either.

I looked around as we were nudged down the path past the metal towers. They looked a little like those electric towers that hold high-tension lines. At the top of each sat an object that I figured was some sort of a miniature radar dish. A spike stuck out of the center of each dish.

I didn't get to see much more, since they took us right into the building. We marched down a long hall, then into an elevator. I could tell we were going down because it took my stomach a moment to decide to follow along with the rest of my body. After a quick trip, the door opened and we were taken along another hallway into a large room filled with all sorts of equipment. It looked like a control room.

There was a man seated at a huge desk. His back was toward us. All I could see above the chair was the top of his head. "Ah," he said, "visitors. How lovely." He turned slowly around in his chair. As he turned, he said, "One should always have visitors on the day one takes over the world."

I didn't pay too much attention to what he was saying. I was struggling too hard to keep from gasping and staring. He was the biggest person I had ever seen. He must have weighed seven or eight hundred pounds. I knew it would hurt his feelings if he thought I was staring at him, so I just looked him in the eyes.

"Allow me to introduce myself," he said. "I am Darius Gastrecco, owner of Gastrecco Worldwide Industries and, very shortly, the ruler of the world." He nodded slightly and smiled.

"I'm Ned, and this is Kevin," Uncle Ned said. He nudged me with his elbow.

"Uh, hi," I said.

Mr. Gastrecco waved his hand around. "Marvelous, isn't it? All of this to generate and control my finest invention — the directable destruction ray."

"Destruction is easy," Uncle Ned muttered. "Try making a life ray."

"I said a *directable* destruction ray," Mr. Gastrecco said, his voice getting louder and his face getting red. He hit the arm of his chair with his fist. "Any fool can make a destruction ray, but mine is directable. Have you any idea how difficult that is? Have you any idea what a masterstroke of genius such a creation represents?"

"Why, yes," Uncle Ned said. "There are all sorts of problems you'd have to solve. For one, the linear propagation of the field is usually proportional to the amplitude of the signal."

I had no idea what he'd just said. But the guy in the chair got excited.

"Exactly," Mr. Gastrecco said. "Yes, you understand what I have done — you can grasp my genius!"

He started talking some more, and Uncle Ned joined in. It was very technical. I knew that if I listened for much longer I'd fall asleep. But they weren't paying any attention to me, so I figured it wouldn't do any harm to explore the place. I wandered to the side of the room. Against a wall opposite the door, there was a computer with a map on the screen. That got me excited. I figured I might be able to find out where we were.

I'd learned a little bit about using computers when I'd stayed with Cousin Amy. It's amazing how easy it is to accidentally erase stuff from the hard drive. I promised myself I'd be more careful this time. Mr. Gastrecco looked like he could yell a lot louder than Cousin Amy. I sat down and clicked the mouse. There were blinking dots at five places on the map. I moved the cursor to one of them and clicked again. At the bottom of the screen, it said, *Washington, D.C.* I clicked on the other spots. The names came up one at a time. There were flashing spots at London, Moscow, Tokyo, and Brasília.

That wasn't getting me anywhere. I glanced over to make sure I wouldn't get in trouble, then tried typing on the keyboard. I knew we were at GWI. So I typed *GWI*. Some numbers came up. A message appeared at the bottom of the screen with something about latitude and longitude. It looked like map coordinates, but I wasn't sure. I tried typing *GWI* again. The same thing happened. Then I noticed that two of the dots had stopped flashing. I typed *GWI* three more times. Sure enough, the other three dots stopped flashing. I tried again, but the message *Reprogramming complete* came up.

I tried a few more things, but nothing happened.

Finally, I gave up and wandered back to Uncle Ned. He was still talking about rays and energy and stuff like that with Mr. Gastrecco.

After a couple more minutes of this, the man looked at a clock on the wall and said, "As much as I am enjoying our conversation, and it certainly has been delightful, I have a schedule to keep. Would you care to watch as I conquer the world?"

"Certainly," Uncle Ned said. But he turned toward me and winked. I guess he didn't think too much of Mr. Gastrecco.

"Ten minutes," Mr. Gastrecco shouted as he looked around the room. "Take your positions. This is not a drill." Then he swiveled his chair back to his desk and pushed a large red button. A monitor rose from the center of the desk.

People were running all around, going to different spots in the room. Some were turning on monitors and others were putting on headphones or adjusting knobs on the control panels.

"Energize the system," Mr. Gastrecco shouted.

Around the room, I could hear the click of switches being thrown. A humming sound started to fill the air — quiet at first, then louder and louder.

"Psssst."

I looked up. Uncle Ned had whispered to get my attention. Then he motioned with his head toward the door. I nodded and we started backing out of the room.

Everyone was so busy running around and doing stuff that they didn't pay any attention to us. When we got out the door, we turned and hurried along the route we'd taken in, going down the hallway to the elevator, then up to the other hallway and out of the building.

"Do you really think he's going to take over the world?" I asked as we dashed to the car. I didn't like the idea of someone doing that, but if Mr. Gastrecco did take over the world I'd at least be able to tell people that I'd met him.

Uncle Ned shook his head. "No, I don't think his destruction ray is going to work."

"How come?"

Uncle Ned started to explain why as we drove back to the gate and away from GWI. I didn't understand much of it, but Uncle Ned had figured out that the ray lost a lot of strength as it went along. The farther away the target was, the less damage the ray could do.

When he finished his explanation, I asked, "How come you didn't tell him it wouldn't work?"

Uncle Ned shrugged. "He really didn't strike me as the sort of person who appreciates criticism. Some folks just don't want to hear about it when they've made a mistake."

"Yeah, I think you're right. It's better if he finds out for himself." I could just picture how Mr. Gastrecco would have acted if Uncle Ned had told him. He'd probably pound his fists a whole bunch and shout a lot. That wouldn't have been very nice. I'd already listened to more than enough shouting in my life.

"Ah," Uncle Ned said as we drove to the top of the next hill. "We can watch from here. You'll probably even be able to see the ray fade in power. It might hit with quite a jolt if the target were nearby. But, from what he told me, he was planning to shoot five rays at places all over the world, including Washington and London."

Washington and London? I thought as the towers started to glow. "Was he also aiming rays at Moscow, Tokyo, and Brasília?" I asked, remembering the names from the computer.

"That's what he told me. I certainly would have tried to stop him if I thought his ray would do any real damage," Uncle Ned said.

The towers started to shake. Then, from all five at once, bright beams shot out and streaked into the sky. That's when I thought about what the computer had said: *Reprogramming complete.* And that's when all five beams changed direction. It was pretty amazing to watch. They turned around in tight curves and streaked toward the five buildings on the ground at GWI.

"Golly," Uncle Ned said, "it really is directable. That's quite an accomplishment." He shaded his eyes against the bright flash as the rays hit the buildings.

I closed my eyes for a moment, too. When I opened them, the buildings were glowing and shaking. People were running out the doors. Even at this distance, I could recognize Mr. Gastrecco waddling from the central building. I never would have guessed someone so large could walk so quickly. The buildings kept getting brighter and brighter. After a minute, nobody else came running out. I guess everyone had left. That was a good thing, because an instant later all five buildings disappeared in giant puffs of smoke.

"Gosh," Uncle Ned said. "The beam sure does pack a wallop up close. I wonder if we should go back and see if they need any help."

"I don't think so," I said. "Mr. Gastrecco didn't seem like the kind of scientist who wants people around right after something goes wrong."

"You know, Kevin, you're quite a bright lad," Uncle Ned said as we pulled back onto the road. "I suspect you're absolutely right. I've always been willing to learn from my mistakes. I think that's the mark of a good scientist. But some folks just can't stand being wrong." He looked over at me and smiled.

"The road," I said, pointing ahead.

We went on. It was starting to grow dark. "Maybe we can find a hotel," Uncle Ned said.

"Anything would be fine," I said.

"There's a sign ahead," Uncle Ned said.

I looked up the road. The sign said FOOD AND LODGINGS — 1 MILE.

"Sounds good," Uncle Ned said. "I'm ready to stop for the night."

"Me, too." I watched for the place. There was another sign that said ENTRANCE. It had an arrow pointing to the right.

"Let's see how it looks," Uncle Ned said. He pulled into a path that led to a small cottage.

The sign in front said GRIZELLA'S GUEST HOUSE. TRAVELERS WELCOME. SPECIAL RATES FOR SIBLINGS.

"How charming," Uncle Ned said as he stopped the car. "Gosh, it looks just like a gingerbread house. Isn't that interesting? I like it when folks take that extra step to make a place attractive."

"Yup." I got out of the car. As I stood up, I sniffed the air. A strong, unexpected aroma filled my nose. Gingerbread. I guess they sprayed something in the air to make it smell that way. Uncle Ned was right — it was nice when people went to a bit of extra effort to make a place special.

At that moment, the door flew open and a woman came down the front steps. She had a broom in one hand. "Guests. How marvelous. Come on in. I just love guests. I'll feed you real good. You're looking a bit thin, but I'll fatten you right up, yes I will." She grinned at us.

"What do you think?" I asked Uncle Ned.

"Seems to me that she really likes people," he said. "Shall we?"

"Might as well." I walked up to the porch. I couldn't help touching the wall. As far as I could tell, it really was gingerbread. That was pretty unusual, but I didn't see where any harm could come of it.

"I'm Ned. This is Kevin," Uncle Ned said.

"Step right this way," the woman said, leading us into the cottage.

Chapter Thirteen
Stuffed

"If I eat another bite, I'll just burst," Uncle Ned said as he leaned back in his chair at Miss Grizella's dining table. We'd just had the greatest meal. She was so eager to feed us that she hadn't even shown us our room yet. The minute we'd walked in, she'd practically dragged us to the table.

"What about you, dearie?" she asked. "More bread?" She held out a dish stacked with slices of bread, each slice covered with a thick layer of butter. With her other hand, she lifted up a pot filled with strawberry jam.

"No, thank you," I said. It looked great, but I'd already had five slices, along with a big slab of roast beef and a huge serving of mashed potatoes with gravy. I couldn't believe we'd found such a fabulous place — especially out in the middle of nowhere.

"Are you sure?" she asked, looking back and forth between me and Uncle Ned. "No more dinner?"

"Nope," I said, fighting to keep from burping.

"It was delightful, but I'm full," Uncle Ned said.

"Then I guess I'll go get the dessert," she said, popping up from the table.

"Dessert?" I moaned.

"We have to be polite," Uncle Ned said. "Just take a small portion. She really does seem to take pride in her cooking."

Miss Grizella came right back, carrying a huge apple pie. Before we could say anything, she cut off two large slices. "Eat up," she said, pushing a plate in front of me and another in front of Uncle Ned.

"Thank you." The pie was delicious. Somehow, I managed to eat the whole slice. By then, I was so full I could hardly even think. I felt like I was nothing but a stomach with legs — a stuffed stomach.

"I'll show you to your room," Miss Grizella said.

We followed her. I had a hard time even getting out of my chair. I was feeling very sleepy, too. By the time we reached our room, I could barely keep my eyes open.

"Right through here," she said.

I went to where she pointed and plopped down on a bed. There was some sort of clang, like a gate being closed, but I didn't pay any attention. A few seconds later, I was fast asleep.

The next thing I remember is hearing Uncle Ned say, "Well, this is sort of unusual."

I opened my eyes and sat up. It was morning. By the look of him, Uncle Ned had also just gotten up. He was examining the front of our room. I saw what he was talking about — it certainly was unusual. Instead of a wall, there were metal bars.

"How interesting," Uncle Ned said. "It must be part of the original building. I guess she decided it would be a fun thing for guests. I've heard of places like this — they keep as much of the old building as possible."

I looked around. It felt pretty chilly in the cottage. Our room was right next to the kitchen. As a matter of fact, it almost seemed to be part of the kitchen. On the other side of the bars, there was a stove that heated the place. It was probably used for cooking, too. I guess the fire had gone out. I walked over next to Uncle Ned and tried the bars. The door was locked.

"Miss Grizella," I called, wondering where she was.

"Sshhhh," Uncle Ned said, putting a finger to

his lips. "She must be exhausted after cooking that huge meal. Let her sleep. We can wait."

I didn't want to wait. I went to the rear wall. There was a window there, but it also had bars. "This sure looks like gingerbread," I said, examining the wall around the bars. I tried to break off a piece, but it was pretty hard. Then I tried biting it.

It was gingerbread. I bit off a couple more pieces. I guess I went a little too far, because several of the bars came loose and fell out. I hadn't meant to break anything. But as long as there was an opening, I thought of something nice I could do to make up for the damage I'd caused. I pulled myself through the window.

"Where are you going?" Uncle Ned asked.

"I want to warm the place up a bit," I said.

"How nice," Uncle Ned said. "I'm sure she'll appreciate it."

I walked around the cottage until I found a stack of firewood. I brought an armful in through the front door and got a nice, hot fire going in the stove. Then I threw in a couple of extra pieces of wood just to make sure the fire would burn for a while. My hands were pretty dirty by the time I was finished. I found a bucket and filled it with water.

I brought the bucket with me back through the window so Uncle Ned and I could both wash up a bit.

"You really are a thoughtful boy," Uncle Ned said.

That's when I heard Miss Grizella coming down from upstairs. "Aha, I hope you slept well," she said. "I have a surprise for you today." She looked at us and grinned. Then she went over to the stove.

I guess I'd gone a bit overboard when I'd made the fire. When she opened the door, all these flames shot out. She screamed and jumped back. Then she held out her arm. The sleeve of her dress had caught on fire.

Luckily, I had the bucket with me. I ran up to the bars and threw the water on her.

The flame went right out.

But she didn't stop screaming. Instead, she got louder when the water hit her. Actually, it sounded more like some kind of bubbling than screaming, but she kept making the sound as she sort of dissolved. In a couple of minutes, she'd turned pretty much into nothing more than a puddle of thick goo. It looked kind of like Aunt Emily's lentil soup.

"Wow," I said, staring at the wet mess that had been Miss Grizella.

"Yeah, wow," Uncle Ned said.

We both climbed out the window, then went around to try to figure out what had happened in the kitchen. "She seems to be gone," Uncle Ned said.

"That's too bad," I said. "I was looking forward

to seeing what she was going to make us for breakfast."

"I'm sure it would have been wonderful," Uncle
Ned said. "As it is, I guess we'll have to settle for gingerbread." He broke off a piece of the wall as we left
the cottage.

"It could be worse," I said as I followed him out the door. "At least she didn't live in an oatmeal house."

Once we got back to the car, Uncle Ned said, "You know, this has been a fun trip, but maybe we'd better think about getting back home. I've really been feeling the need to return to my work."

I'd been dreading this moment. How could I tell him I didn't know the way back? Even worse — if we ever got back, was he just going to dump me like all the other relatives? Maybe that's why he was in such a rush to get home. I'd messed up so many things since I'd moved in with him. I'd gotten the wires wrong on the life ray and sprayed us in the eyes with the tire stuff and gotten us lost. I was sure Uncle Ned wouldn't put up with much more. I wondered what would happen to me. There wasn't any place left for me to go. I'd run out of relatives. I'd have to start living with strangers and ruining their lives.

"Home? Let me check," I said, picking up the map.

"Take your time. But see if you can find a good route."

"I'm looking." It was hopeless. I spent as much time as I could staring at the map, rattling it, folding it different ways, looking for anything that might have been one of the places we'd visited. Finally, I accepted the fact that it was no use. I was just going to have to tell Uncle Ned that we were lost.

I put down the map and looked out at the road. For the first time in ages, we were coming to a fork. The road split left and right.

"Which way?" Uncle Ned asked.

I glanced to the right. The road ran straight off into the distance. It looked like it ran into a regular highway. If I squinted, I could just make out the shape of large green signs. From the highway, it would be easy to find out where we were and make our way home. But then our trip would be over. And I didn't know if I wanted it to end.

I looked to the left. The road turned and twisted, going up the side of a mountain. At the very top of the mountain, there was a large castle. As I stared at the castle, a huge bird — maybe a vulture — took off from one of the turrets and flew away.

I pointed to my left. "That way," I said. "I think that's the way we need to go to get home."

"Good enough," Uncle Ned said. He turned onto the left fork and we headed toward the mountain.

As we reached the base of the mountain, we passed a lake. A giant shape started to rise out of the water on the right side of the road. It looked like some kind of sea creature with a long neck. The head lunged at the car as we drove by, just missing us. I looked back. The creature was watching us. It had moved its head across the road, blocking the path behind us.

"Did you see that?" I asked Uncle Ned.

"See what?" He turned toward me. "I've been trying to keep my eyes on the road."

"Never mind." I pointed toward the road.

We definitely couldn't go back now. As I looked ahead, a bolt of lightning struck the castle. I wondered if I had just sent us somewhere we shouldn't be going.

Chapter Fourteen
Sew What?

The trip up the mountain took longer than I'd expected. The road was narrow and full of sharp curves. By the time we got near the top, a heavy rain was falling.

"Maybe we should stop," Uncle Ned said.

"There?" I asked, looking at the dark form of the castle, barely visible through the rain.

"Why not? We've had pretty good luck so far everywhere we've stopped. People have been very friendly."

Another bolt of lightning hit nearby, lighting up the castle for an instant. We pulled close to the entrance, then ran from the car to the huge wooden door. There was no sign of a bell or a knocker, so Uncle Ned pounded with his fist.

"Maybe nobody's home," I said.

We were just about to leave when the door opened. On the other side, lit from behind by light from deeper in the castle, a dark figure greeted us.

"Please come in," she said.

"Thank you," Uncle Ned said. "We thought we should get out of this storm."

We went in through the doorway. The woman stepped back. I could see her now. She looked about Uncle Ned's age and she was very pretty. There was something familiar about her. It took me a moment to realize what it was. Her eyes reminded me of Uncle Ned's. They had that same look, giving me the feeling that her mind was running around in a million different places at once.

"I'm Frankenstein," she said, introducing herself. "Doctor Felicia Frankenstein."

"I'm Ned, and this is Kevin," Uncle Ned said. "Are you a medical doctor?"

She smiled. "By training, yes. But I don't see patients anymore. Not living ones, that is. I've dedicated myself to discovering the secrets of life and death."

I heard Uncle Ned gasp when she said this. I could also almost hear the twang of Cupid's bow as my uncle got an arrow in his rump. I could almost see bluebirds and hearts circling his head. I could almost hear thousands of violins playing sappy music in the background. I could almost throw up.

"Yes, life!" Uncle Ned exclaimed. "That's my quest, my goal, my burning and consuming mission."

He started to tell her about his life ray.

She started to tell him about her experiments. Then she dragged him off to her lab. I was left standing there, not sure whether to follow. I waited for a while, then went down the steps they had taken. Ahead, I could hear them, still excited, talking about their successes and failures.

"I'm so close," Dr. Frankenstein was saying. "I know I'll succeed this time. But if I had help, then there's no way I could fail. Could you stay for a few days?"

"Certainly," Uncle Ned said. He turned to see me standing in the doorway. "Kevin, we're going to stay for a bit."

"Sure." I looked around. The lab was filled with tons of electrical equipment. There was a huge table in the middle of the room. There was a sheet on the table, and something under the sheet. I looked back at Uncle Ned. He and the doctor had started talking again. He seemed excited. I left them and headed for the stairs.

"Kevin," Dr. Frankenstein called as I went up, "the kitchen's down at the end of the hall to the left.

Help yourself if you're hungry. And feel free to explore — we might be down here for a while."

"Thanks." I went up the steps.

Food did sound like a good idea. All I'd had since morning was some gingerbread. I went down the hall and found the kitchen. There was a refrigerator in the corner. I spotted some peanut butter and a package of cheese behind a big glass jar. I took the jar out and put it on the counter, then grabbed the cheese.

I found some bread in a drawer and made a cheese sandwich. I took it with me as I started to explore the castle. It was pretty interesting. There was a tower on one side. I climbed to the top. From there, I could see all around the mountain. The road we'd come up ran down the other side through a small village.

As I stood in the tower, looking down the mountain, I realized we should have taken the other road. We'd be on our way home, then, just Uncle Ned and me. Now, because I'd led us up the mountain, it looked like he'd found someone else — someone who shared all his interests.

When I came down later — I'm not sure how long I'd been in the tower, but it must have been hours — they were still in the lab. "Want some food?" I asked.

"Oh, thanks, Kevin, but I think we'll stick with what we're doing for a while longer," Uncle Ned said.

Dr. Frankenstein looked up from her work. "I have a pretty good library upstairs," she said. "I'm sure you could find something to read."

"Okay." I'd hoped that they were going to ask me to help, but I guess they didn't need me. I went up again and found the library. There was a ton of science books. But there were also lots of other things, including some interesting-looking novels. I pulled out one called *First Men on the Moon*. It was kind of old-fashioned, but it was also pretty good. I read for a while, then fell asleep.

In the morning, I went looking for Uncle Ned. He was still in the lab with the doctor. "Good morning," I said.

"Morning?" Uncle Ned looked around. "Goodness, I guess we worked all night."

"But we're almost done," Dr. Frankenstein said. "We're ready for the brain." She turned to me. "Kevin, could you go get the brain for us?"

"Sure," I said, feeling good that they were asking for my help. "Where is it?"

"Upstairs," she told me. "In the refrigerator. It's in a big glass jar. You can't miss it."

"Uh, is there just one jar in the fridge?" I asked, hoping she'd say there were a whole bunch. I couldn't remember whether I'd put the jar back. As I thought about it, I was pretty sure I'd left it on the counter.

She shook her head. "Good brains are hard to come by. It's the only one I have. Be very careful with it."

I went upstairs to the kitchen. The jar was sitting on the counter next to the fridge. I felt it. The glass was warm. I looked at the brain. It seemed fine, but I really had no idea what a spoiled brain would look like, and I sure wasn't going to sniff it. I brought the jar down, wondering why everything that was easy to break always felt so slippery.

"Thank you, Kevin," Dr. Frankenstein said. "You've been a great help. Tonight, with luck, we give him life. I hope you'll join us."

"Sure." I watched for a minute as Uncle Ned took out the brain and put it on a tray. He didn't seem to notice that it wasn't cold.

Then I went back up to the library to read some more. I didn't mind. I was used to being by myself. At least Dr. Frankenstein had some good books.

That evening, Uncle Ned called me down to watch the final part of the experiment. "This is fascinating," he said. "She's taken a very different approach. I've been working on a single dead creature at a time, while she's been trying to assemble life from separate parts. Fascinating."

I followed him to the lab. Outside, I could hear a thunderstorm coming. Dr. Frankenstein pulled a lever and the table with the body rose up in the air. Then she stood, looking up toward the ceiling. Uncle Ned stood next to her. I noticed that they were holding hands. Seeing that made my stomach feel funny.

There was a flash from outside, followed by a bang so loud it seemed to explode inside the room.

The wires leading down to the table started jerking and wriggling like snakes. The air filled with the smell of high voltage. Three more lightning bolts slashed into the wires. Then everything fell silent. Dr. Frankenstein pushed the lever. The table came down. She reached for the sheet.

The body moved. It sat up. I stared into its face — a face sewn together from parts. The creature swung its legs from the table and slowly stood, rising above us. It must have been more than seven feet tall.

"I guess I got the proportions a bit wrong," Dr. Frankenstein said. "I knew I should have measured things."

"But you did it," Uncle Ned said. "It's alive."

"Yes," she said, "it's alive."

The creature staggered, taking an awkward step, then another. It shuffled toward me, nearly toppling forward. It stopped inches from me. It looked down. I looked up. I looked into its bloodshot eyes and open mouth and I knew what it wanted.

"I ate all the cheese," I told it, "but there's some peanut butter, and the bread's not bad. Come on, let's get a snack."

I turned and headed toward the kitchen. The monster followed, but it walked pretty slowly. I guess it needed to learn how to make all the parts work together. I waited at the top of the steps. For a moment, as it was coming up, we were eye to eye. Then I was back to being the smaller guy.

I went to the kitchen and got out the peanut butter and the bread. "Here," I said, handing it a sandwich. "Eat up."

The sandwich lasted about three seconds. When it was done eating, I realized that I couldn't keep thinking about it as a monster. It needed a name. "Kevin," I said, pointing to myself. Then I pointed to the monster. I hoped its brain wasn't so damaged that it couldn't understand me.

"Ggrrrraannnnfffldddd," the monster said.

"Granfeld?" I asked.

The monster shook its head and said, "Rrrnnnnnngggg."

"Randal?"

"Rrrrnnnnngggggllll."

"Ringo?"

"Rrrnnnnggggggllldddd."

"Ronald?"

"Uuuhhhhhhhhhhnnnn."

"Ronald? That's your name?"

"Uunnnnhhnnn," Ronald said again, nodding his head yes.

I felt pleased that I had been able to understand him. It was tough, but if I listened carefully, I was sure I'd get pretty good at it. Maybe he'd be okay even though I'd left his brain out for so long.

"Kevin," I said, pointing to myself again. Then I pointed to Ronald and said his name. I figured it was good to repeat the lesson. That's what my teachers always did. They repeated something until everyone understood it. Actually, some of them repeated it until I thought I'd scream, but I guess that's how things get taught.

Ronald looked at me for a moment, then walked over to the sink and got a glass of water. He swallowed it in one gulp. He got another drink, then moved his jaw around. Then he said, "Ah, that's better. Dreadfully difficult to speak after eating peanut butter, don't you think?"

"Uh, yeah."

"Pleased to meet you, Kevin."

"Your brain is okay?" I asked.

He nodded. "It's funny — the last I remember, I couldn't think very clearly. My mind was just wandering off in all sorts of directions and was always filled with too many distractions. But that little problem seems to have cleared itself up."

"Good. That's real good." I finally relaxed.

"So, what's there to do for fun around here?" Ronald asked.

"There's a library. And there's a neat tower. You can see the village from there."

Ronald shrugged. "I'm not much for reading. But I love villages. I think I'll go terrorize this one." He walked toward the door, then looked back. "You coming?"

"That doesn't sound like a good thing to do," I said.

"Hey, it's fun. Come on. We'll knock down a few walls, scare the local folks, shout and grunt a bit. We'll send them running and screaming. What do you say?"

I shook my head.

"Suit yourself," he said. He turned and walked off.

I ran down the steps to the lab. Uncle Ned and Dr. Frankenstein were still hopping around congratulating each other on their success.

"I hate to interrupt," I told them, "but I think we have a problem."

Chapter Fifteen
Together We Split

"What's wrong?" Uncle Ned asked.

"Ronald said he was going to go terrorize the village," I told them.

"Ronald?" Dr. Frankenstein asked.

"That's his name. He had some peanut butter, then said he was going off to the village."

Dr. Frankenstein shook her head. "This always happens. Do you have any idea how many times someone in my family has been chased out of her home by a mob of angry villagers? I've lost count."

"Big problem?" Uncle Ned asked.

She nodded. "The Frankenstein family has always had villager trouble. I don't understand it. We try to be good neighbors, but sooner or later an angry mob always shows up, tears the place apart, and sets it on fire with their torches."

"Maybe we can catch him before he reaches the village," Uncle Ned said.

We rushed up the stairs and started down the hall. As we ran past the library, a voice called out, "Hey, what's all the excitement?"

I stopped and looked in. Ronald was sitting there, reading a book. "Weren't you going to the village?" I asked.

"What's the matter, Kevin?" he asked. "Can't you take a joke?" He laughed and went back to reading his book.

I got back at him the next day. I put eggs in his shoes. Then he hid peanut butter sandwiches in all my jacket pockets. We became great friends right away. Good thing. Since Uncle Ned and Dr. Frankenstein were spending all their time discussing her next experiment, I really didn't have anyone else to talk to.

That evening, right after dinner, Ronald came lumbering into the library. He was getting better at walking, but he still tended to crash into things. "Villagers!" he said. "There's an angry mob coming."

"Yeah, right." I didn't even look up from my book. I'd fallen for a couple more of his tricks, but I wasn't about to fall for another. It was bad enough that he'd fooled me with the one where he pretended to take his thumb off.

"Look for yourself," he said.

"I still don't believe you," I told him. I got up and went to the tower. From the top, I could see points of flickering light. There were villagers, lots of them, carrying torches and rushing up the road toward the castle.

"Maybe we should tell the others about this," I said.

"Good idea."

We went to the lab. "There's a mob of villagers headed toward the castle," I said.

Dr. Frankenstein stomped her foot. "I knew it. I just knew it. Well, maybe we should go elsewhere for a few days."

Uncle Ned nodded. "Kevin and I are familiar with that concept." He paused for a moment, then said, "I have a fabulous idea. Let's go back to my home. It should be safe by now."

"Wonderful," Dr. Frankenstein said.

I wasn't sure I liked the idea. Now that he'd found her, he'd probably dump me as soon as we got back. I'd had at least three other uncles dump me when they met someone they really liked. Well, actually, Uncle Manny was angry about a couple of other things, too. Especially about the time I tried to use his false teeth to pull some nails out of an old board. I never would have done it if I knew the front teeth would snap off so easily. I tried gluing them back. Just my luck we had corn on the cob that night.

I guess Uncle Hector was annoyed about me spilling hair remover on his champion poodle. And, to be honest, Uncle Eric was probably not happy about the Jell-O in the swimming pool. But all three of them might have kept me if they hadn't met someone else.

I thought about it as we rushed to the car. Things were looking grim. Uncle Ned even made me sit in the backseat with Ronald. Dr. Frankenstein got to sit up front.

"We'd better go back to where the road splits," I said. "I don't think we want to go near the villagers."

"Sounds like a good plan," Uncle Ned said. He started to head down the twisting mountain road. Then he looked over at Dr. Frankenstein and asked, "You say this has happened before?"

She grabbed the wheel, pointed ahead, and said, "The road."

"Oops." Uncle Ned got control of the car again. Dr. Frankenstein looked back at me and winked.

I sat with Ronald and talked. Behind us, I could see the torches of the villagers. They were going into the castle.

"Mob violence never solved anything," Ronald said.

"Yeah," I agreed. "Say, do you like comic books?"

"Sure."

We sat there, comparing our likes and dislikes

while Uncle Ned drove toward the bottom of the mountain. But as we got near the lake, I remembered the thing that had risen from the water.

"Keep an eye out up ahead," I said.

A second later, Uncle Ned hit the brakes. The creature was blocking the road, its long neck rising from the lake. I looked through the rear window. Dozens of the villagers were coming down the road toward us.

"I'll see what I can do," Ronald said, reaching for the door handle.

"No," I said, grabbing his shoulder. As big as he was, I knew he was no match for the creature ahead of us. I leaned over the front seat and opened the glove compartment. The apple was still there — the one I'd gotten from the woman dressed like a witch back in Amlack. If I was right, it would do the trick. I rolled down my window and said, "Here, catch." Then I tossed the apple at the creature.

It snapped the fruit right out of the air. I waited. For a moment, nothing happened. Then, the whole neck went limp and the head dropped back beneath the water. I figured it would probably sleep for a hundred years, unless a prince came along and kissed it.

Uncle Ned drove on. We soon left the angry villagers far behind.

As we got on the highway, the fog got real heavy. After a while, we couldn't see anything. Uncle Ned

went slowly. I had no idea how long we were driving before it started to get light outside. I guess I napped a bit. Finally, as the sun was coming up, the fog lifted.

"Hey, this looks familiar," I said.

In a few minutes, we were at the outskirts of town. We were home. Well, Uncle Ned was home. I wasn't sure where I would end up. As we drove down the street toward Uncle Ned's house, he said, "Kevin, I have to tell you something. Felicia and I were talking, and it involves you."

"Here it comes," I muttered.

"We're getting married," he said.

"Congratulations." I tried to sound happy for him.

"And, if it's okay with you, we'd like you to stay with us. We want to adopt you."

"Really?" I asked.

"Really," Uncle Ned said, turning around to look at me.

Dr. Frankenstein grabbed the wheel before we could drive off the road. "Watch the car, Ned," she said.

"Oops." Uncle Ned turned back, but he kept talking. "Of course we want to adopt you, Kevin. I couldn't imagine life without you around. You're very special."

"Or you, Ronald," Dr. Frankenstein said, looking back.

I tried to say something, but my throat felt too tight for the words to get out. It looked like I was going to get a family, complete with a big brother — a really big brother — and a mom and dad and a home.

I glanced down at the floor next to my feet. I

couldn't say everything I wanted to say — not yet. But I could show them how I felt. Yup, it was still there. "Here," I said, handing Dr. Frankenstein the bouquet of daisies that the hitchhiking girl had left behind. They were still fresh. I had a funny feeling they would stay that way forever.

"Thank you, Kevin."

I looked across the street at the cemetery. Everything was quiet over there. That was a relief.

"We're home," Uncle Ned said as we drove up to the house. He turned around and put his hand on my shoulder. "You did great with the map, Kevin. I'm real proud of you."

"Thanks." I pointed ahead and said, "Watch the road."

"Oops." Uncle Ned turned his attention back to the last few yards of our trip. He pulled past the hedges into the driveway. I heard a screech as Uncle Ned hit the brakes and said, "Oh, boy."

I stared out the window. Then I said, "Oh, boy," too. The front yard was crowded with living dead people. They were all around the house. Some were sitting on the porch. There were a couple up on the roof. I had the feeling they'd been waiting for us. The moment we turned into the driveway, they all started walking toward the car.

Before Uncle Ned could back out, we were surrounded by a large circle of living dead.

"I'll handle this," Ronald said. He got out of the car and shouted, "Get away. Scat. Scram. Shoo."

The creatures moved closer.

"I mean it," Ronald said. "Right now. Get out of here. Don't make me tell you again." He stomped his foot.

The living dead stepped even closer.

There was only one chance. I grabbed my jacket from the car seat and searched the pockets. "Ronald!" I shouted. "Here." I tossed him a peanut butter sandwich and hoped he understood what I had in mind.

Ronald took a huge bite, chewed for a second, then opened his mouth wide. "Gnarrrlllll!" The cry rang out.

It worked. All the living dead turned and ran off.

Except they ran into the house. I'd messed up again.

"Kevin," Uncle Ned said, "do you realize what this means?"

"Yeah." I nodded. I knew exactly what it meant. We couldn't go home. I was a failure. I was a total disaster who wrecked everything.

"This is fabulous," Uncle Ned said.

"What?" I asked.

"This is our first real success." Uncle Ned clapped his hands together. "The ray works better than we thought. And it all happened because you crossed the wires. This is promising. And they didn't look very angry at all. Maybe that part wears off." He turned toward Dr. Frankenstein. "What do you think?"

"The poor dears," Dr. Frankenstein said. "They looked scared. They were probably trying to be friendly. We shouldn't have chased them away."

"Yes," Uncle Ned said. "We'd better go make sure they're all right."

I watched as Uncle Ned and Dr. Frankenstein headed up to the porch. Hand in hand, they strolled into the house. I realized there was nothing to worry about. They knew what they were doing. I figured I might as well join them.

"Coming?" I asked Ronald as I got out of the car.

"Narrrggff," Ronald said.

"I think there's some milk in the fridge," I told him.

He grinned at me.

I grinned back, imagining Ronald's face when he tasted milk that had been sitting around for so long. Then I walked up the steps and went into my home. Life was good. Life was a bit strange, but life was good.

About the Author

David Lubar lives in Pennsylvania with his wife, daughter, and cats. He likes good books, silly jokes, pizza, extreme roller coasters, pinball machines, and monsters. He especially likes writing for kids. He's worked as a magazine editor, video game designer, and computer programmer. His other books for Scholastic include THE ACCIDENTAL MONSTERS series. More than anything else, he really hopes you enjoyed *Monster Road*.